The Best of

LORI WICK

A Gathering
of Hearts

HARVEST HOUSE PUBLISHERS

EUGENE, OREGON

Cover by Dugan Design Group, Bloomington, Minnesota

Cover photo © Collage Photography / Veer

THE BEST OF LORI WICK...A GATHERING OF HEARTS
Copyright © 2009 by Lori Wick
Published by Harvest House Publishers
Eugene, Oregon 97402

ISBN-13: 978-1-61523-905-4

Printed in the United States of America

A Note from the Author

Each book is a delightful labor of love, and I feel blessed and privileged to bring the characters and their faith, relationships, and discoveries to life on the page. Every time I finish a novel, it's hard to say goodbye to these people and places. Whether it's shy Cassandra reading to a blind, handsome stranger in England in 1812 or McKay Harrington watching with amusement and fear as Callie nearly starts a fire in her Colorado cabin while making breakfast, I miss writing their stories and the things I learned in the process. Yet they really live on each time a reader picks up a book and gets lost in the tale.

That's why I'm excited to share this gathering of special moments from the hearts of my characters and from their stories. I had great fun reflecting on my old friends in these pages. Whether you're meeting them for the first time or revisiting favorites, I hope that you will be entertained and encouraged by this special collection of memories.

May these stories celebrate the journey of faith, love, gratitude, and joy that you and I experience in our lives.

From my heart to yours,
Lori

Love

Girl Talk

The girls shared a very feminine room as well as a large, soft bed, and as usual, ended the evening with talk about the day.

"Do you love Robert, Eddie?"

"Yes," the older girl said softly. "I think I loved him right away but then thought it must be a crush. Then after we started to write each other, I knew it was real."

"Do you get excited about living in a house that he built for the two of you?"

Eddie only laughed. Her mind hadn't gone that far.

"I'm never going to fall in love," Jackie declared as she got comfortable on the pillow. "I think men are a pain."

"You might change your mind, Jackie," Eddie said gently.

"Never! I'm still amazed that you spoke to that Clay Taggart today. I just hate him."

Eddie smiled as she rolled to turn down the lantern but didn't speak. She was still thinking, *You might change your mind, Jackie.*

Desire realized is sweet to the soul.

PROVERBS 13:19

A First Kiss and a Second Chance at Love

Amy's heart melted within her as his lips touched hers, and Silas felt as though his own heart was going to pound through his coat as she leaned closer and didn't pull away.

One second they were kissing and the next second Amy was gone. Silas stared up at her from his place on the log. She had leapt up and was staring at him with tortured eyes, her hands clenched so tightly together that her knuckles were white. Silas stood and reached for her as he spoke.

"Amy, please—"

"Don't touch me, Silas—just don't touch me."

Standing in front of the log and holding his place, Silas spoke. "Amy, you must know how I feel. You must know that my feelings for you are deep. And you, Amy, what about you? Please don't ask me to believe you don't feel anything for me."

"Of course I feel something for you. We're friends." The words sounded foolish and inane even to her own ears, but Amy couldn't seem to help herself.

Silas looked furious. "Is that what you were just now when you let me kiss you—a friend?"

Amy shrugged helplessly, not even knowing herself why she had allowed the kiss. Silas drug off his cap, and Amy watched him rake his hand through his hair, his frustration more than evident. Suddenly Amy felt angry and frustrated too.

Taking him completely by surprise, Amy boldly stepped forward and pushed as hard as she could on his chest. Normally he would have hardly noticed the relatively slight pressure she put on him, but he was so surprised by her action that he took a step backward, forgot the log, and fell over it and onto his back.

"What did you do that for?" he bellowed from his undignified sprawl on the ground.

"Because you've ruined everything. We were such good friends, and you've just ruined it," Amy cried in pure frustration.

Silas was off the ground in an instant, knowing his brother Paul had been right. Even as Amy had shouted at him in rage, he had seen the fear written across her face.

Amy retreated as he came toward her, and Silas stalked her until she was backed up against a tree. His expression was fierce but his voice was calm. "Take a good look at me, Amy Nolan, a very good look. I am *not* Thomas Blane. I am *not* going to declare my love for you and then marry someone else."

Silas' look grew extremely tender as they both stood still, his eyes drinking in the woman he loved. He cupped her face within his big hands before he spoke his next words. "I love you, Amy. I love you as I've never loved anyone. You would but need to crook your smallest finger in my direction and I would gladly carry you down this hill to the parsonage and make you my wife today."

There is no fear in love; but perfect love casts out fear.

1 John 4:18

Afraid to Love

Y ou've fallen quiet, Rusty."

"Just thinking."

"About Mr. McCandles?"

"Yes."

"Is your heart being affected in all of this, Rusty?"

"I think it is, Mother. I'm not sure how I feel about that."

"Shall I tell you how I feel?"

"Oh, please do."

"I don't think you should fight this, Rusty, even if it means letting yourself fall in love."

"Oh, Mother."

"Come here, dear." Jackie needed her oldest child closer. "Come so I can see you."

They had been side by side on the davenport, but Rusty moved until Jackie could put an arm around her. Jackie spoke again once she'd pulled Rusty close and cradled her cheek with her free hand.

"Did I frighten you?"

"No, but it's a little shocking when someone so perfectly speaks my thoughts."

"What did I say?"

"That I'm afraid to let myself fall in love with him. It's the truth, Mother."

"Why does it frighten you?"

"Because I'm afraid he won't love me in return. But worse than that, I'm still afraid he might not be a good father. I couldn't stand that."

Jackie pulled Rusty's head down close and rested her cheek on the top of her head. *What do I say, Father? I can't promise her that Mr. McCandles will love her, although I suspect he already does. I can't tell her just to throw caution to the wind; she must think clearly on this. They haven't known each other very long. Help me to be wise and careful with my words. I fell for Clayton so swiftly, but it was years before we had each other. Help me, Lord, and help Rusty to know her heart but never to forget Yours.*

"We are never to worry, Rusty," Jackie said softly. "That's a much easier thing to say than to practice. If you are fretting about your feelings or whether he'll be a good father, you must confess your lack of trust. God has so much better for us than we ever do for ourselves, and His yoke and burden are light. Did that make sense?"

"Perfect sense. Thank you." Rusty paused again. "How would you feel about Mr. McCandles in the family, Mother?"

"If you love him, and you both want to build your relationship and family in Christ, I think it would be wonderful."

Rusty sighed, a huge load lifting from her heart. For some reason she needed her mother's permission; and not just her permission, but her approval with God's standard behind it. She knew if she kept this in mind she could not go wrong.

"You're feeling better already, aren't you?"

"Yes. I needed to hear those words."

Jackie pressed a kiss to her brow. "I'm glad, but I must be honest with you and tell you that your hairpins are putting a hole in my cheek."

Rusty sat up with a surprised laugh. Jackie joined her. By the time the men gained the drawing room, the women were both flushed with giggles.

> *Peace I leave with you; My peace I give to you;*
> *not as the world gives do I give to you.*
> *Do not let your heart be troubled,*
> *nor let it be fearful.*
>
> JOHN 14:27

Faith

Delighting in the Word

SEAN DONOVAN

Charlie directed her attention to the gift Sean had placed in her lap. The whole room erupted with laughter at the way she babbled after the gift was unwrapped.

"Oh, Sean; oh, my! My very own Bible! I can't believe it! Do you know how badly I've wanted one? Where did you find this? Oh, look at the pages! Isn't it beautiful? I can't believe it—my very own Bible!"

Charlie moved to her husband's chair and threw her arms around his neck. He laughed as she tried to squeeze the life from him. She thanked him repeatedly and had to stop herself from sitting down to read it right on the spot.

Sadie went to ready the cake and coffee after the presents were put aside. Charlie joined her in the kitchen, giving the younger woman a chance to mention her Bible.

"You must wonder how I could be so excited about receiving a Bible," Charlie began tentatively.

"It has crossed my mind that there's been a change in you," Sadie said matter-of-factly.

"I'd like to tell you about it sometime, Sadie."

The older woman turned her full attention to her niece. She studied the fervent young face for a moment and tried to put her finger on the change. At first she had attributed it to having a happy marriage with a handsome husband and a baby on the way, but Sadie could see there was more.

"This means a lot to you, doesn't it?" Sadie asked quietly.

"Yes, it does."

Sadie suddenly smiled. "Well, honey, if it means that much to you, I'll listen to all you have to say."

They were not given any further time for talk, but Charlie praised God for opening a door. Even as the cake was served by Sadie's capable hands, Charlie prayed about the future opportunity she would have to speak with her aunt.

When Sean and Charlie did head home, Charlie immediately sat down to read her Bible. She had read Sean's on many occasions, but this was somehow special. As always, Charlie prayed that God would show her just what He would have her see as she read the words, but she never dreamed of the things she would discover in the weeks to come.

Your word is a lamp to my feet
and a light to my path.

PSALM 119:105

A Complete Heart

Silas' relationship with Amy was good, if not as comfortable as it once was. Silas smiled wryly to himself at the different way a man thinks of his little sister and the way he thinks of the woman he wants for his wife.

Little things he had never noticed about Amy before were becoming very dear to him: the way she chewed her lower lip whenever she was anxious about something; the way her voice took on a childlike quality as she prayed, so trusting and sweet; her concentration and sparkling eyes whenever she played the piano. These and so much more made up the whole of Amy.

Amy. Amy Cameron. Silas had tried the name out loud one day in the barn when there was no one to hear but the cows. He loved the way it sounded, but not knowing if it would ever come to pass was disheartening. He tried not to dwell on it.

He petitioned God constantly to give him strength and wisdom in this situation where he felt so helpless. Silas was unable to see it right now, but this time in his life was bringing him closer and closer to God.

There were even moments when he felt God had forgotten him, but they were brief. For even amid the pain of wishing for a life with Amy and not knowing if he would ever have it, was a sweet, peaceful knowledge that God had not deserted him and that His will for Silas was perfect and complete.

But as for me, I will watch expectantly for the LORD;
I will wait for the God of my salvation.
My God will hear me.

MICAH 7:7

The Fruit of a Woman's Faith

So you think that if a person is saved it will be evident?"

"Yes. I didn't always. I mean, I tried to tell myself that if a person told me he had made that choice then I should believe him, but James puts it very well in James 2. He says I'll show you my faith by my works. If the conversion is real, my darling, then the whole world should be able to tell."

"Oh, Mother," Jackie said, taking her hand. "It's never been like this. I want to pray all the time, and I love it when someone reads the Bible to me. I've always been so bored and restless with church, but I can't wait until tomorrow."

Addy leaned over and put her arms around Jackie, her heart so full that she couldn't even speak.

Now all these things are from God,
Who reconciled us to Himself through Christ
and gave us the ministry of reconciliation.

2 CORINTHIANS 5:18

The Witness of a Prayer

Abby, do you really believe God can hear you? I mean all those things you said to Him about taking care of your family and healing Mr. Cameron. Do you really think God can do all of that?"

Abby was quiet for a few minutes, and Ross wondered what she was thinking. He would have been surprised to find out she was praying.

"Ross, I'm glad you felt you could ask me," she finally began in a gentle voice. "I'm not ashamed of my belief in God, so I'm not upset that you heard me pray. When I was a little girl, my grandmother died. I cried and cried for days, but my grandfather never shed a tear.

"It took me some time, but I finally asked him why. He told me that he and my grandmother had grown up together and one day a traveling preacher came to town. The man said that Jesus Christ was God's Son and that He had died on the cross for sinners. Well, my grandpa said he knew he was a sinner and needed a Savior and that day he believed on Jesus Christ. He said Grandma believed that day too, and he knew she was with Christ and that's why he didn't cry. He was going to see her again.

"He asked me that day if I had ever made that decision, and I had to say no. He wanted me to pray with him right then and tell God of my sin and believe He died for me, but I said no. A few years later my grandfather lay on his deathbed, and I went in to be near him. There was no fear on his face because he knew where he was going. Jesus was his Savior, and Grandpa was going to be with Him and see Grandma again.

"Before my grandfather died that day, I knelt by his bed, and with his hand holding mine I told God of my need for a Savior. The Bible says to 'believe on the Lord Jesus Christ and thou shalt be saved.' Well, Ross, I did believe and I've never been the same.

"The God of all creation lives inside of me, and without Him I am nothing. I grew up in a home where prayer—talking with God—was a daily occurrence. Jesus Christ is my best friend, and when I pray, I pray believing He loves me and His will for me will be perfect. It was hard to lose Ian, but I know it was God's will and that I'll see Ian again."

Abby was sure she had rambled on too long. It was Ian who was the preacher, not she; Ross would be thoroughly confused.

"How can I know your God?"

Abby couldn't believe her ears. She had been so absorbed in the recounting of her story, she had missed the look on Ross' face. It was a look of wonder and searching. Abby wanted to throw her arms around him.

Let your speech always be with grace, as though
seasoned with salt, so that you will know how
you should respond to each person.

COLOSSIANS 4:6

Comfort and Peace

"Close your eyes," Edward commanded, taking the cup from her grasp.

"Every time I do that, I see that awful man."

Edward took a breath. It had been terrible.

"He would have robbed you," he said at last. "And he might have killed you. You did what you had to do."

Niki nodded, suddenly very ready to close her eyes. She lay still for a long time and then heard pages turning next to her. She peeked over at Edward and found him bending over his Bible.

"Does something in there comfort you?"

"Yes," he answered softly.

"What is it?"

"I'm reading in Genesis—the first few chapters about creation."

"And this brings comfort to you?"

Edward looked over at her. "After an incident like that, I need to be reminded of the orderly God who loves me and who would never let me out of His sight."

Niki sat up a little. "And you get that in Genesis?"

"Yes. You see, God's design and plan are perfect. He doesn't let things happen without a reason. I may never know why we were stopped today, but God had a plan, and I can rest in that."

Niki had to think on this one. Edward stayed silent.

"But there are verses that speak of comfort?" Niki asked, leaning toward him a little.

"Yes, many of them, especially in Psalms. Would you like me to find some?"

"You don't have to." Niki caught herself and pulled back, emotionally and physically.

Edward ignored her and turned to that book. He began in chapter 119, reading several verses.

"'This is my comfort in my affliction; for thy word hath quickened me.' That was verse 50. Then verse 76 says, 'Let, I pray thee, thy merciful kindness be for my comfort, according to thy word unto thy servant.' A verse from chapter 86 doesn't use the word comfort, but the message is still there. 'For thou, Lord, art good, and ready to forgive, and plenteous in mercy unto all those who call upon thee.'"

"How do you know of those verses?"

"I have them marked in my Bible."

"So you've studied it quite a bit."

"Off and on for many years," he answered honestly.

"What's been most significant to you?"

Edward cocked his head to think.

"It's probably the fact that salvation is only the beginning. Once we trust Christ for our eternal destination, we still have a life to live on this earth. I spent too many years living for myself and not really seeking what God would have of me."

"So eternal life might have been lost to you?" Niki asked.

"No, my salvation, the trust I put in Christ to save me, was real, but I was ignorant and blinded by my own desires about living for

Him. I would not have been lost, but neither would I have been able to stand before God and say that I'd chosen to devote my life in order to live as His child. By that I mean making Him my God in every sense.

"I can think of God as my Savior and even my friend, but I must never forget that He is God, and after He saves me, I must put myself in subjection to Him and His will."

"How long did it take you to learn all of this?"

Edward smiled. "Quite a while, but He's a most patient God."

I will say to the LORD, *"My refuge and my fortress,*
my God, in whom I trust!"

PSALM 91:2

Joy
and
Laughter

Barnyard Humor

Kaitlin and Jeff had been seated in the living room with Bill and May for just a few minutes when Rigg and Marcail came in from outside where they'd been seeing the barn.

Marcail sat next to her sister on the sofa, and Rigg took a place on Marcail's open side.

"You should see the barn, Katie!" her sister told her with enthusiasm. "They have four horses, but one is old and tired; they use him for burning hay."

Kaitlin laughed along with everyone else at Marcail's description. "I think what they meant was that he's too old to work, so all he does is eat. That's a hay burner."

"I think Loni's brother must be a hay burner, but he's not that old."

The Taylors watched as Sean and Kaitlin exploded with laughter. The brother Marcail spoke of was 19 and very lazy. They had never heard it put that way before, but it was very fitting.

We do not want you to become lazy,
but to imitate those who through faith and patience
inherit what has been promised.

HEBREWS 6:12 NIV

Accidental Charm

There wasn't a time when Pup came into the cabin that she didn't trip on the threshold. She knocked pans from the stove and bowls from the table. She spilled water and food down the front of herself daily. She was an accident waiting to happen. "Clumsy little pup," must have been the phrase that started the nickname for Callie, and McKay could see why. But what most fascinated him was that Pup herself seemed completely unaware that anything was amiss.

If he lived to be a hundred, he would never forget the morning she set a kitchen towel on fire. It didn't burst into immediate flames, but did smoke and flame slightly before she noticed it. At first McKay was too stunned to react, and about the time he was ready to open his mouth and warn her, she had spotted it. She made a face that showed the inconvenience of it all and calmly poured some water from the pitcher to douse the fire. The room was a little smoky after that, but she only opened the front door. She didn't turn to him with any type of apology but went back to the meal preparations. She wiped at the mark that it made on the stovetop but never referred to it again.

It had been two weeks and four days since he'd been shot, and tonight was the first night McKay was going to join Pup at the dinner table. As he sat in his usual place on the sofa, however, the burned towel incident strongly in his mind, he wondered if this was safe.

"Are you getting hungry?" Pup interrupted his thoughts as she entered the cabin carrying a basket. She tripped but never dropped a thing.

"A little. I thought I would come to the table tonight."

"Suit yourself," she said mildly.

When he saw Pup putting plates and flatware on the table, he rose. He was acutely aware of his bare feet and uncombed hair, but his hostess took no notice. Sitting opposite of where he'd seen her sit, he saw with pleasant surprise that she'd made muffins. McKay spoke when Pup joined him at the table.

"I don't wish to be presumptuous, but would you mind if I returned grace?"

"No."

Her tone didn't indicate any emotion, so taking her at her word, McKay bowed his head.

"Heavenly Father, I thank You for this day. I thank You for Callie's hard work on the meal and for the care she has given me. I ask You to bless us this evening and protect us through the night. Amen."

"Amen," Pup agreed softly, and then passed the bowl of rabbit stew to her guest.

They dished up in silence, but soon McKay commented, "My mother makes rabbit stew. It's my father's favorite."

"It's tastier than squirrel."

"I think so too."

All other attempts at conversation fell flat. McKay resigned himself to eating in silence just as he bit into his second muffin. With the food still in his mouth, a shudder went all through his body. Pup noticed and stopped eating.

"Are you in pain?"

McKay pulled the muffin away from his lips. Hanging from the muffin was most of an eggshell. Pup scowled at it.

"I wondered where that went," she said blandly before passing him the basket so he could take another.

McKay shook his head no and forced himself to chew what was in his mouth. The crackle of shell was a bit hard to take, but he chased it all down with water. The drink made him feel slightly better, but another little piece in his teeth caused a second shudder.

He wondered when he would stop being surprised by Callie Jennings.

Do not be worried about your life, as to what you
will eat...Look at the birds of the air,
that they do not sow, nor reap nor gather into barns,
and yet your heavenly Father feeds them.
Are you not worth much more than they?

MATTHEW 6:25-26

Queen of Hearts

Lizzy, Cassandra, Tate, and Morland sat around the card table, talking over a game of ruff.

"She's got a great hand," Morland said, watching Cassandra arrange her cards.

"How do you know?" Tate asked.

"She always bites her lip when she has so many good cards she doesn't know what to play first."

"Not fair, Morland!" Cassandra scolded him, still studying her hand. "You're giving away old family secrets."

"Well, if I didn't, you just did."

Cassandra ignored him and played trump.

"What did I tell you?" Morland said as he and Tate both surrendered cards.

"We shouldn't have let them talk us into these teams," Tate observed.

Lizzy smiled, just short of laughter.

"That settles it," Tate put in. "We're going to mix things up next time."

More competitive than Tate would have imagined, the women shared a smile. In the next hour they outscored the men three out of four times, and the men were crying for revenge.

"But you can't really get revenge unless you remain a team and beat us," Cassandra said, her voice a little too sweet.

"That's not going to work," Tate said, not falling for it. "And to make things more interesting, I think Lizzy should be my partner, and you should be Morland's."

Both women laughed at his nerve but agreed. Morland quietly went along, but he knew he got the better end of the deal. For all her unworldly ways, Cassandra was a dab hand at cards. The team of Cassandra and Morland thrashed Lizzy and Tate in less time than it had taken the women on their own.

"I should have warned you," Lizzy said to Tate, not sorry in the least. "Cassie always carries me. She's so unassuming, we get away with it every time."

Cassandra did her best to look innocent, but Tate was not fooled.

"I shall have my revenge," he promised. "I tell you that this is not over yet!"

The occupants of the table laughed at him before Lizzy rang for tea. They put the cards away, and Henry joined the four of them as they visited over hot cups of tea and biscuits.

The evening ended all too soon, both women taking the stairs at a slow pace.

"I do believe I'm in love, Cassie," Lizzy said quietly.

"I would never have guessed."

"And you?"

"I'm still mulling it over."

Lizzy laughed. "The only thing you're mulling over is what type of dress you want."

The women hugged goodnight and went their separate ways, but it was a good long time before either of them slept.

Delight yourself in the LORD; and He will
give you the desires of your heart.

PSALM 37:4

Gratitude and Thanksgiving

Thankful for One Another

You never did say what you were the most thankful for in Paul's life."

Grandma Em stopped her peeling and looked thoughtful. "I guess I'm most thankful he went to seminary school. It was no easy decision, I can tell you. He was so unhappy at the ranch. He considered going into medicine. He even went out with Mark a few times, but it just wasn't for him. His letters home are filled with the joy of the Lord. So I guess I'm thankful he's where he's supposed to be and happy about it."

The women went on with their dinner preparation. The turkey was cooking and the potatoes were peeled. Christine was working on pumpkin and mincemeat pies. Both Julia and Susanne were bringing dishes so that everything would not be left to Grandma Em and Christine.

"You never asked me what I'm thankful for today."

Grandma Em looked surprised. "You're right, I didn't. Will you tell me now?" she asked kindly.

"I'm thankful for you," Christine answered with her head down, her voice quiet and thick with tears as she rolled out the pie dough. She stopped when she felt Grandma Em at her side. The women hugged and cried silently for a time.

"Do you remember how awful our first meeting was?"

"Yes, I was scared to death of you."

Both women found this all highly amusing. So when the Mac-Donald family entered a few minutes later, it was to find Christine and Grandma Em with the giggles, their eyes still wet with tears.

What thanks can we render to God for you in return
for all the joy with which we rejoice before
our God on your account...?

1 THESSALONIANS 3:9

All a Man Needs

In the main house at the ranch, Cash was looking for his wife.

"Reagan?" Cash called to her as he mounted the stairs toward their room. She didn't answer, but he found her sitting on the side of their bed.

"Hi," he said as he sat down next to her.

"Hello," she said, still giving him her profile. Her voice told him she was thinking.

"What's up?"

"I was just thinking about your Christmas gift" she admitted, finally meeting his eyes.

"What about it?"

"I couldn't stand for you not to like it, Cash, at least not in front of anyone else." She turned to look at him. "I want to give you your gift now."

"Now?" Cash started to laugh. "Reagan, I know I'll like it." He tried to reason with her for some minutes, but she had that stubborn tilt to her chin.

"I want to give it to you now." Looking like a conspiratorial child, Reagan took his hand and led Cash quietly down the stairs. At the bottom she peeked around the corner, and when it was clear, rushed him to the room where the gift was hidden.

Cash was laughing so hard that he tried to hold his breath. Reagan darted inside, shut the door, and leaned on it, breathing theatrically.

"What are we doing?"

"Shh," she told him. "They'll hear us."

Cash found himself dragged along to the closet. It creaked a little when it opened, and even Reagan started to laugh.

"Come on," she urged him, having picked up a lantern. "Come through here and close your eyes."

"It's dark, Reagan," he said indulgently.

"I know, but I'm going to light the lantern. Are they closed?"

"Yes." He heard the strike of the match.

"Okay," she said, watching him carefully. Cash opened his eyes and then blinked.

"You bought me my own bike?"

"Yes. It's taller than mine. It should fit you very well." He walked toward it like a child on his tenth birthday. Reagan watched him, her hands clasped in front of her.

"You bought me a bike," he said with such pleasure that Reagan beamed. "Look at me. I'm a city boy!" Watching as he tried to straddle it in the tiny room, she suddenly realized what she'd done.

"Oh, no," she suddenly said. "You like it!"

"That's bad?"

"No, but now I don't have anything to surprise you with for Christmas."

Cash set the bike aside and came to her. His arms were gentle around her as he gathered her to his chest.

"My entire family is coming for Christmas in the home I share with my new wife, and you think I need more gifts?"

Reagan threw her arms around his neck, her lips seeking his

own. She suddenly felt exactly the same. He was all the Christmas gift she would ever need again.

> *God is able to make all grace abound to you,*
> *so that always having all sufficiency in everything,*
> *you may have an abundance for every good deed.*
> 2 CORINTHIANS 9:8

Eternal Gratitude

How is your father?" Lydia asked Anne.

"Much the same, I'm afraid. Not that well."

"How do you keep from growing discouraged, Anne?"

"Some days I don't, but on days when I'm thinking well of the situation, I keep reminding myself that God is in control and that He loves my father and me very much.

"Please don't misunderstand me, Lydia. Life is not easy, but we never go without. I don't have a parent I can confide in, but I have many people who are available for me. Mine is an easy situation to pity, but pity is not necessary. I think that it's easy to look at someone else's situation—a more painful situation—and somehow comfort ourselves in that. But should we be looking any further than eternity?"

"I'm not sure I know what you mean," Lydia had to admit.

"My father isn't well, but I have eternal life," Anne explained. "I have to walk most places even when I'm tired or hot, but I have eternal life. We don't live in a beautiful home any longer, and we've lost our estate, but I have eternal life. If I view my situation by just looking at my own life, I do better than if I start comparing it to someone else's in order to find comfort or something to be thankful for."

Lydia thanked her for the reminder. She had asked about her father, thinking it might do Anne some good to talk about him, and it turned out she had been the one to hear something she needed. Often busy with five children, Lydia was at times tempted to feel sorry for herself. Not many days ago, she had done just as Anne cautioned against, reminding herself that things could be worse. It was far better to find joy and peace in all that God had already given her.

Let the word of Christ richly dwell within you,
with all wisdom teaching and admonishing one another
with psalms and hymns and spiritual songs,
singing with thankfulness in your hearts to God.
Whatever you do in word or deed,
do all in the name of the Lord Jesus,
giving thanks through Him to God the Father.

COLOSSIANS 3:16-17

Marriage

A Much Better Arrangement

Gone were the chairs that had sat before the fire. In their place was the sofa, long and inviting. Rebecca's eyes flew to Travis where he sat at one end, his legs stretched out. He was smiling at her, his eyes watching her every move. Rebecca couldn't help but laugh. She giggled from deep in her chest, a sound of delight and relief. Travis had been waiting to hear that sound. A moment later he snatched her hand and pulled her into his lap. He kissed her long and hard, but then broke the kiss and held something aloft. It was a simple gold band.

"Be my wife, Rebecca?"

"Another ring," she whispered.

"The one you should have had six years ago."

"Oh, Travis."

She watched as he tugged her ruby ring free of her left hand and tried to slide the band in place. She had to help him.

"Do you want this on with it, or on the other hand?"

"The other hand," she replied instantly.

Travis examined both of her hands when the rings were in place and then kissed the back of Rebecca's ring hand. He then cuddled her against him.

"Do you know what I wish?" he asked softly.

"What?"

"That I'd moved this sofa weeks ago."

Rebecca would have laughed all over again, but Travis was kissing her. She could feel the weight of the gold band on her hand even as she was very aware of the man who held her.

His wife. I'm going to be Travis Buchanan's wife.

> *Husbands, love your wives, just as Christ also loved*
> *the church and gave Himself up for her.*
>
> EPHESIANS 5:25

An Eye for Love

I tell you, they're ideal for each other."

A romance between Pup and McKay had never entered Nick's mind, so there was no feigning the confusion on his face.

"Ideal for what?"

"Marriage," Camille said simply, her face alight with pleasure. "What could be more perfect?"

Nick shook his head and scrubbed at his ear. He couldn't have heard her right.

"You mean Pup and McKay?"

"Of course."

"Camie," he began patiently, "that's not going to happen."

"How do you know?"

"Because I know," he retorted with complete conviction. "McKay is a dedicated treasury man, and Pup is the best undercover agent I've got."

"And those things mean they can't fall in love?" Camille's voice rang with skepticism. However, Nick was not swayed.

"It doesn't mean they can't; it just means they won't."

Camille was reminded for the thousandth time in their marriage that men and women simply didn't think alike. And to Camille's way of thinking, it was too bad. There would be so much more they could all get done if husbands would just go along with their wives' plans. Settling back against the pillow, Camille let the matter drop. She would have been outraged, however, if she could have heard her husband's thoughts.

Standing in the closet, he pulled the belt from his waistband and reached to unbutton his shoes. He wanted to laugh but refrained. *Pup and McKay! What a joke. I love you Camie, but sometimes you definitely have more beauty than brains.*

> *But for Adam there was not found a helper*
> *suitable for him. So the LORD God caused a*
> *deep sleep to fall upon the man, and he slept;*
> *then He took one of his ribs and closed up*
> *the flesh at that place. The LORD God fashioned*
> *into a woman the rib which He had taken from*
> *the man, and brought her to the man.*
>
> GENESIS 2:20-22

Never a Dull Moment

Is Christine going to marry Uncle Luke?"

"Why do you ask, Calvin?" Julia asked as she dried her face.

"They were holding hands on Sunday, and Uncle Luke smiles a lot."

"Yeah," Charles joined in. "He plays with us, but his eyes are always watching Christine."

"Well, I think that Luke and Christine care for each other, but marriage is a big step, and until they decide what they want and share it with us—" Mac paused here to make sure he had both boys' attention—"we are not going to ask them or bring the subject up. Understood?" Both boys nodded solemnly. "Okay, go get bundled up. We've got some shoveling to do."

The boys' shouts and laughter echoed back to Mac and Julia's ears as they ran for their room.

"What's the frown for?"

"Well, you just told the boys we're not going to ask Luke and Christine what's going on, and I was hoping you would talk to Luke and find out how he feels."

"Julia, my sweet, that is none of our business." Mac's voice was patient.

"I know! That is precisely why I was trying to figure a way to find out." She stated this so matter-of-factly that Mac burst into gales of laughter. Julia hit him with a pillow, but to no avail. He was still chuckling after he was dressed and ready to leave the room.

He bent over Julia, who was buried beneath the covers in bed, his face close to hers.

"Do you know what I'm thankful for?"

Julia smiled, sure she would hear a loving endearment.

"I'm thankful that being married to Julia means never being bored." Mac kissed the tip of her nose and scooted toward the door. He slipped out an instant before another pillow sailed through the air.

He who finds a wife finds a good thing
and obtains favor from the LORD.

PROVERBS 18:22

A Guy Smitten

I 'm in love with a woman who can't cook." Rigg spoke softly even as a smile came over his face. He froze when he heard steps behind him.

"It's not like you to talk to yourself, Rigg," Jeff said quietly. "Want me to leave?"

"No, come on in." Rigg watched as his brother folded his long frame into a chair. He dwelt briefly on the fact that the young ladies at church were very attracted to Jeffrey Taylor but he never responded in kind. It looked for a time as though Jeff might be headed for trouble where girls were concerned, but something had happened when Jeff was still a teen that seemingly changed him forever.

Rigg knew his younger brother to be as desirous of a wife as he was and wondered how Jeff was feeling about what he'd just overheard. He decided to ask him.

"I think the word infatuation fits a little better than love does, Rigg."

"You think it's too soon for me to be in love then?"

The younger man shifted uncomfortably over the vulnerable look on his brother's face. He, quite frankly, thought the world of his older brother and it was hard to see him unhappy. And then there was Kaitlin. It was not at all hard to see why Rigg believed himself to be in love.

"You started working in this store, Rigg, when you were only 14. And then Uncle Leo turned the whole thing over to you at 19. You haven't had any time to date girls or even spend much time with them and now Kaitlin Donovan comes into town and knocks you right off your feet. Naturally you assume it's love. Maybe it is. I don't know."

Jeff felt that he'd said enough and watched Rigg's face carefully to see if he'd upset him. When Rigg finally spoke, Jeff wished he had made him angry. Rigg was more upset than he was letting on, and Jeff didn't want anything unresolved between them.

"Well, I doubt if you came by to discuss my love life. What did you need?"

"Rigg?" Jeff's voice was pained.

"No, Jeff it's all right. I *do* feel like I'm in love. But Kaitlin isn't ready for anything like that, and having to explore these feelings on my own is a hurting thing."

"And I just made it worse by saying you're not even in love."

"It's all right, Jeff." Rigg suddenly smiled. "I'll just make you eat those words at the wedding."

Jeff laughed. This was the Rigg he knew, confident and purposeful.

So Jacob served seven years for Rachel and they seemed to him but a few days because of his love for her.

GENESIS 29:20

Prayer

Gratitude Leads to a Life of Prayer

I've never felt this way, Travis," Lucky admitted. "I know you go to church, and Margo's mother tries to pray, but I've never felt anything toward God—not really. And then last night I held Sarah Beth. She cried and cried, and I wanted to cry myself. I wanted to thank God for letting her live. I don't know where the thought came from, but I still want to."

"I'd be happy to pray with you right now, Lucky. We can take time right this minute to thank God for sparing Sarah Beth."

Lucky gawked at him. "You don't have to be in church?"

"No. God is everywhere, and He delights to hear the voices of the people who have made Him their Lord."

The young cowboy's look sobered. "I haven't done that, Travis. I haven't ever prayed before."

"God already knows that, Lucky, and He takes it very seriously, but He loves you anyway. I can pray if you'd like."

"You can do it for me?"

"Well, I can't commit your life to Him—you would need to do that—but I can thank Him for sparing Sarah Beth."

Lucky nodded. "Should we get on our knees?"

"It's awfully cold, Lucky. The Lord will understand if we stay on our feet."

Again Lucky nodded, his heart pounding. At the last moment he remembered to remove his hat.

"Father in heaven," Travis began, his voice utterly normal, "I thank You that Lucky is my foreman. He works hard and is an asset to this ranch. I also thank You that You've given him Margo and Sarah Beth. You have blessed him greatly, Lord, and for the first time Lucky is seeing this. I thank You, Father, that You saved little Sarah's life. We could be praying near her grave right now, Lord, but You had other plans. I thank You that she is still with us and that Lucky understands Your hand moved or she would not be here. Please continue to show Lucky what You would have him know about You, and help him to listen. I pray these things in Christ's name. Amen."

Travis opened his eyes to find Lucky staring at him.

"You just talk to Him, Travis," he said, his voice amazed. "I didn't think it was that easy."

"It is after you've accepted God's gift of salvation."

Lucky nodded. He was feeling so overwhelmed he could hardly speak.

Oh give thanks to the LORD, call upon His name;
make known His deeds among the peoples.
Sing to Him, sing praises to Him;
speak of all His wonders.

1 CHRONICLES 16:8-9

The Patient Prayers of a Grandmother

Paul was careful in not getting too close to anyone. The men he worked with knew nothing about him, so they had no way of knowing that this morning's mood stemmed from a dream about Corrine—not the smiling, beautiful Corrine of the first few days of courtship, but the Corrine of the last days, pale as the sheets she lay on, so still and near death...Paul shoved the thoughts aside and continued on into the trees.

Paul's family would have been hard put to recognize the man he had become. His hair was long, obviously having not seen a barber since he'd left Baxter, and a full, dark beard covered his face. But the biggest change was in Paul's personality. Gone was the carefree youth with the sparkling blue eyes with whom they had grown up. Gone was the dedicated man of God they had watched him become. In his place was an angry, bitter man who believed his life was over because he felt dead inside.

There wasn't a day that passed when Paul did not hear the voice of God beckoning to him. Paul was fast becoming proficient at pushing such thoughts aside and going about as he pleased. However, he had promised his grandmother he would stay in touch. So upon arriving and getting work in the logging camp, he had written her a brief note.

"Gram," it stated simply, "I'm on a logging crew in Hayward. Please do not watch for me. It's going to be a long time, if ever, before my road leads home again. Paul."

Paul had no way of knowing that his grandmother held that letter in her hand every day and prayed for him, and that many nights as the moon flooded through the window in her bedroom, she would fall asleep looking at it on her bedside table.

As for me, far be it from me that I should sin against
the LORD by ceasing to pray for you;
but I will instruct you in the good and right way.
Only fear the LORD and serve Him in truth with all your heart;
for consider what great things He has done for you.

1 SAMUEL 12:23-24

Trusting Enough to Let Go

He'll be here before you know it, and then you'll know your heart. He'll either be everything you remember and more, or your heart will be cold."

"What if his heart is cold toward me?" Eddie couldn't keep the tremor from her voice.

Addy smiled. "If that was the case, he wouldn't be taking a southbound stage to see you."

Both girls suddenly smiled at their mother. When Addy stood they lay down, dark heads finding comfortable places on the pillows and their mother tucking them in as she had when they were young. Addy moved to Jackie's side first, pulling the covers high and then bending to kiss her. She received a surprisingly tender hug for her efforts before moving to Eddie's side. They kissed and embraced as well before Addy turned the lantern down and moved to the door. Her soft "Goodnight, my darlings" floated over them like a warm caress.

Once in the hall, the door closed behind her, Addy trembled from head to foot.

He's going to come and claim her heart, Father, and I don't know if I can stand the separation. He's going to take my Eddie, and even though I see the love in her eyes whenever Robert's name is mentioned, I'm not ready to let her go.

Morgan had fallen asleep in his chair downstairs, but Addy

didn't go back down. She moved further along the upstairs hallway and into their room to ready for bed. Her movements were laden. She was tired, and that always produced exaggerated emotions. She knew that sleep was her best option right now. As her own head lay on the soft pillow, and the light quilt settled around her, Addy said another prayer.

Help me to remember how far You've brought us, Lord. Help me to remember to trust as I've done before. You love Eddie more than I do. Help me give her to You. Robert too.

> *May the God of hope fill you with all joy and peace*
> *in believing, so that you will abound in hope*
> *by the power of the Holy Spirit.*
>
> ROMANS 15:13

Daily Prayer

The women worked well together. They prepared and ate a quiet breakfast. Christine rose afterward, intending to clean up the dishes, but Grandma Em waved her back to her seat. "This is part of my morning routine, Christine." Christine watched her reach for a large black Bible. She opened the book and began to read aloud, giving Christine no time to be embarrassed or to comment.

"'Give ear to my words, O LORD; consider my meditation. Hearken unto the voice of my cry, my King and my God, for unto thee will I pray. My voice shalt thou hear in the morning, O LORD; in the morning will I direct my prayer unto thee, and will look up.' Psalm 5:1-3."

Grandma Em closed the book and bowed her head. "Dear heavenly Father, I praise and thank You for the beautiful day You have given us and the blessings You daily give us. May we be mindful of You and ever in Your service."

Grandma Em continued to pray, but Christine opened her eyes to see if anyone else was in the room. The only people she had ever heard pray were the preachers at her parents' funeral and later at her grandfather's. But neither one had sounded like this. Grandma Em made it so personal, as though God were right in the room with them. With another quick look around, Christine closed her eyes again.

"And Father, I thank You for Christine. She is already so precious to me. Having her here has brought added sunshine to my life. Please bless and keep her and give us a special day together. In Christ's name I pray. Amen."

Christine, having never had a person pray for her, did not know what to say. To her surprise, no words were necessary.

The righteous man will be glad in the LORD and
will take refuge in Him;
and all the upright in heart will glory.

PSALM 64:10

Romance

Holding Hands, Holding a Gaze

Y ou're doing fine." Ross spoke the soothing words as he held Mandy's hand and led her out to the middle of the pond. He turned suddenly and skated backward, taking both of her hands in his and guiding her progress.

"I thought you said you hadn't skated for years!" Accusing him, she watched him glide backward, seemingly without effort. The words were a mistake because they caused her to take her eyes off of their feet. In the next instant both skates went in different directions. Ross caught her as she started down, laughing at the surprised look on her face.

"That was close," Mandy said breathlessly.

"You didn't think I would catch you, did you?"

"No, I guess I didn't."

"O ye of little faith," teased Ross. And then, "Amanda, look at me."

"If I look at you, I'll fall," Amanda insisted and kept her eyes glued to the ice. Nothing he could say would make her raise them.

"You're going to get a stiff neck," Ross finally told her, but she had no chance to reply because Becca and Eliza skated into them just then and all four went down in a laughing heap.

"Becca, I thought you were going to stay with Silas."

"I was, but Eliza's helping me."

"I can see that." The skeptical tone was lost on the little girls who were once again on their skates and making unsteady progress across the pond with shrieks and giggles.

"Ross, wouldn't you rather move a little faster? I mean, just because you asked me to come with you doesn't mean you have to hold my hand the entire afternoon."

"Maybe I want to hold your hand the entire afternoon." He had her on her feet now and they stood still for a moment on the ice. Mandy loved the way he looked in his hat, especially when he pushed it back a bit on his forehead, like it was now.

Ross thought Amanda, with her white hat slightly askew, was the most adorable thing he'd ever seen. He slipped one glove off to brush a few flakes of snow on her cheek. She never took her eyes from his as he replaced his glove and took her mittened hand, not even when Ross guided her forward across the ice.

Bright eyes gladden the heart;
good news puts fat on the bones.

PROVERBS 15:30

Never Want to Lose You

Dakota used the kitchen door because he knew it would be open, and surprisingly enough found his boss, Brace, sitting at the table reading the mail.

"Well, Dakota, when did you get in?"

"Only just. Where is Darvi?" Dakota felt he had waited long enough.

"In the living room. Right now she's reading a letter from your mother."

"*My* mother?"

"Yes," Brace responded, looking very pleased as he answered. "It was a pretty thick envelope. I suspect she's telling Darvi every rotten thing you did as a child."

Dakota had heard enough.

"Darvi," he called firmly as he moved that way, not missing the sound of someone scrambling and papers crackling. He went through the dining room, and sure enough, the living room was empty.

"Darvi." His voice was coaxing now, even as his eyes searched for some sign of her. It took some doing to spot a bit of her skirt sticking out from the door that opened into the dining room.

He moved the door slowly and tried not to laugh at her attempt at an innocent face.

"Dakota! When did you get in?"

He came close and put his hands on the wall on either side of her head.

"Just now."

"How nice," she said a little too brightly, all the while keeping her hands behind her back.

His eyes dropped down for a moment before coming back to hers.

"A little bird told me you got a letter."

"A letter?" Darvi appeared to think on this. "Now, let me see. Have I received any letters lately?" With that Darvi couldn't hold on. She laughed and brought out several pages.

"Is this really from my mother?"

"Yep," she teased him. "Every word. I'm learning an awful lot."

For a moment they just stared at each other. Darvi felt her cheeks grow warm and tried to divert his gaze with a question.

"Do you know when you head out again or where you'll be going?"

"No. And no."

Darvi playfully shook her head. "You don't know much, do you?"

"I know that I love you," he said softly.

For Darvi, time stood still. She had never pushed this man to say those words, but she had been feeling love for him for a very long time.

"When did you decide this?" she asked.

"When I was near the river. It reminded me of the night we stayed on the trail and you met the rattlesnake."

"And that made you love me?"

He nodded. "It caused me to remember how many times I could have lost you. I don't want to lose you, Darvi. Not now—not ever."

Her heart filling her eyes, Darvi said, "I love you, Dakota Rawlings."

Moving slowly, Dakota leaned forward and kissed her. Darvi sighed when he pulled away. Dakota wanted to kiss her again but told himself that would have to wait.

"Brace tells me you're headed home next week."

"Yes, I prayed you'd get here before I left," Darvi admitted.

"This time you'll leave knowing that I love you."

Darvi smiled. "And you won't forget my love, will you?"

"Not a chance."

This time Dakota didn't kiss her but took her gently into his arms. It was the sealing of a promise that both of them would keep.

Let Your lovingkindness, O LORD, be upon us,
according as we have hoped in You.

PSALM 33:22

A Sincere Proposal

C hase walked Rusty up the stairs and to her door where she turned and looked up at him. A moment later he bent his head and kissed her softly on the mouth.

"I haven't said I would marry you." Surprised as she was, Rusty felt the need to remind him.

"I must be more aware of that than anyone, Rusty...my Katherine."

"Then why the kiss?"

Chase's eyes traversed her face, as if memorizing every detail. "Before you stands a man who's desperate to show you that he's not trying to secure a mother for his child."

Rusty sadly shook her head.

"Why can't you believe that, Katherine?"

Her hands moved helplessly; she saw no help for it but to tell him. "I don't think you even find me attractive," she said softly. "Maybe when I wear my hair up, but that's not very often. Sometimes you seem exasperated with my ideas, and I think you see me as something of a child. I couldn't live in a marriage like that, a marriage of convenience so you'll have a live-in nanny for Quintin. I want children of my own, lots of them.

"I also think you must find me a very shallow person, but I'm not. I give much more thought to things than you think I do. It's true that I make mistakes and look on life as an adventure, but just because I have the heart of a child when I play with one doesn't mean that I'm a child myself."

"Oh, Katherine," Chase whispered—he'd never known such pain.

"It's all right." She knew she needed to release him before he could say another word. "I understand. I would never hold you to your proposal."

Chase was too stunned to move or he'd have taken her in his arms.

"I love you, Katherine," he said softly.

Rusty stared at him.

"And it's all my fault that you don't know that. I haven't been the same since I stood at the train station and looked up to see you coming toward me."

Rusty couldn't believe what she was hearing.

"I should have told my mother when she arrived that the timing was terrible, and that I needed to be alone with you. We could have gone into town for the day or even taken the train to Manitou, anything that would have given us time so I could do this properly."

Rusty was still speechless.

"You see, I knew then that I had found a woman to love and marry. I even asked your father when they were here that weekend if he would object to my approaching you. He told me that he approved as long as you did, but I didn't want to rush you."

Rusty licked her lips. She could hardly breathe.

"I didn't plan to overwhelm you tonight as I have, but will you tell me one thing?"

Rusty nodded yes.

"Are you open to hearing more from me on this subject, or do you wish to tell me right now that you never want marriage mentioned between us again?"

Again Rusty licked her lips. "A real marriage?"

"Oh, yes," His voice had grown even softer. "With *many* children."

"You love me?" She had to make sure she'd heard him right.

"So very much."

Your wife shall be like a fruitful vine within your house,
your children like olive plants around your table...
Thus shall the man be blessed who fears the LORD.

PSALM 128:3-4

Family

The Sweet Joy of Belonging

A Place Called Home

Well, if that isn't the most depressing sight I know— seeing my dress on another woman and having it look better on her!"

Christine spun around in surprise upon hearing these words. Her eyes met those of a beautiful, dark-haired woman.

Julia Cameron MacDonald stood with her hands on her hips trying to look disgusted, but the smile in her eyes told Christine the truth. Julia stepped forward then, hand extended and a full smile lighting her face.

"I'm Julia MacDonald. Gram tells me your name is Christine." Julia shook Christine's hand and both women felt a spark of comradeship. Their relaxation was visible as all doubts cleared.

"Yes, I'm Christine Bennett, and thank you for the dress. I hope it hasn't put you out."

"Julia has enough dresses to loan the entire town and not be put out."

It was a man's voice coming from the kitchen doorway that Julia had just vacated. He was the size of a mountain. Christine stared at him, thinking it was the first time she had met someone bigger than her grandfather. But Julia spoke to him as if she were scolding a child.

"Behave yourself, Mac. Come over here and meet Christine." She caught his hand and pulled him over. "Mac, this is Christine Bennett. Christine, this is my husband, John MacDonald, Mac for short." Christine's hand was swallowed in a huge paw that she could not keep from staring at. Mac, seeing the train of Christine's thoughts, said, "My mother always tells me I just didn't know when to stop growing." He smiled before adding, "I can't say as I meet too many women the height of my Julia." Mac dropped an arm across Julia's shoulders and gave her a quick hug.

Christine smiled at Julia. "I was rather surprised when Susanne brought me a dress that actually fit. You can't know how much I appreciate it."

The next hour was spent in dinner preparation and conversation. Christine met Calvin and Charles, Julia's sons. They had their mother's dark hair and their father's expressive brown eyes.

Content with family surrounding her, Grandma Em bustled around, finishing the table with a hug here and a word there. Christine was again amazed at how accepted she was. When Susanne and Mark arrived, Emily bounced into the kitchen to hug Christine and inform her of her upcoming fourth birthday. Then she raced off to find Calvin and Charles.

Dinner was wonderful—with only one embarrassing moment. Mark prayed, thanking God for the day, the food, and the addition of Christine to the family. Immediately on the heels of the "Amen," Emily wanted to know if Christine was now a member of the family because she was wearing Aunt Julia's dress.

Seeing Christine's flaming cheeks and Mark about to reprimand

Emily, Grandma Em broke in kindly and explained that Christine was family because they loved her and wanted her to be.

Ruth said, "Do not urge me to leave you or turn back
from following you; for where you go, I will go,
and where you lodge, I will lodge. Your people shall
be my people, and your God, my God."

RUTH 1:16-17

Part of God's Family

How's this, Mandy?"

"Oh, Carrie, you look so pretty!"

The two sisters stood in front of the mirror in Mandy's room and looked at the changes in each other. They were considerably filled out from head to foot. Their faces were fuller and shining with health.

Carrie was built much the same as Mandy, petite of height but just a shade slimmer. She looked adorable this evening in her lavender dress with short, puffed sleeves and rounded neckline. Amy had helped pull her hair up, and the effect was darling with her slim neck and nearly bare arms.

Mandy's dress was light pink and set off the darkness of her hair and eyes. The waistline was nipped in and the bodice fitted. Mandy was thrilled that she no longer looked so straight up-and-down. Her own neckline was modestly rounded with a ruffle around the edge and sleeves longer than Carrie's, but the lightweight cotton fabric made her outfit very cool and comfortable.

"Mandy, I've been wanting to talk with you and I haven't had a chance. Can we talk now?"

"Of course," Mandy answered, even though she knew that Carrie was going to tell her about her new religion. What Mandy didn't know was that the words Carrie had chosen were going to affect her tremendously. They sat on the edge of the bed facing each other.

"We're family, Mandy," Carrie began without warning, speaking quickly lest she lose courage. "And nothing can ever change that. I think we're closer than most sisters, and I wouldn't want it any other way. But I realized after we moved in with Silas and Amy that there was another family I wanted to be part of and that's God's family.

"I don't think there's ever been anything that we haven't shared in, but this—" She stopped for a moment, afraid that Mandy would be angry with her.

There were tears in Mandy's eyes, and it was almost too much for Carrie. She knew Mandy was hurt, but her soul was more important than a few earthly tears. "Mandy, I love you," she continued softly. "That won't ever change. Today is my birthday, but I wasn't really born until last Sunday when I told God I needed a Savior."

Mandy was speechless. Carrie's face shone with contentment and peace. This wasn't some religion, some Sunday morning ritual. This was a changed life.

While we have opportunity, let us do good to all people,
and especially to those who are of the household of the faith.

GALATIANS 6:10

A Surprise Lullaby

At the top of the stairs, Marcail hesitated.

"I didn't brush my hair or put on my shoes."

"Your hair is lovely," Alex said as he took her hand. "And since we don't stand on ceremony around here, you don't need your shoes unless your feet are cold."

Marcail wondered at the lovely feeling that spiraled through her over his words and the way his long fingers curled around her own.

Supper was another uproarious affair, and Marcail loved it. It reminded her of meals with Rigg's family. After the dishes had been cleared, the group converged on Helen's room for a game of Sticks.

Marcail was unfamiliar with the game, but she learned that it was something of a family tradition with the Montgomerys. She also learned the reason it was new to her: Helen had invented Sticks herself. The family had been playing it for years.

The game consisted of a huge stack of cards with questions or commands printed on each and dozens of small wooden sticks. Marcail was rather lost at first, until someone explained that the person with the most sticks at the end of the game was the winner.

Helen was in her element as she handled the cards. The questions ranged from easy for the children to outrageous for the adults. The cards that resulted in the most fun were those with commands. The players laughed until they cried when Skip had to stand on his head and say the pledge of allegiance, but everyone had to forfeit a stick when he did so without laughing. At times it seemed that Helen made up the rules as she went along, but she was always fair.

As the evening neared an end, Skip, Alex, and Hannah had the majority of the sticks. Marcail was beginning to tire when Helen called her name as the next turn.

"All right, Marcail," Helen said with a determined look in her eye, "sing us a song in a foreign language."

"Oh, Mother," and "Oh, Grandma," were the sounds around the room. Marcail looked surprised at everyone's reaction until Susan spoke.

"That's mother's favorite question, Marcail. She's been asking it for years, and no one has ever done it."

Marcail's face was neither mischievous nor triumphant. The look she gave her mother-in-law was tender as she began to sing a Hawaiian lullaby she'd learned in the Islands. Her voice was high and pure and sweet, and the room was utterly still even after she was finished.

The room remained silent as Skip, Alex, and Hannah stood and gave *all* their sticks to the newest member of the family.

O sing to the LORD *a new song,*
for He has done wonderful things.

PSALM 98:1

Love

The Rest of Our Lives

Bobbie," Jeff said tenderly as he took her arm. "We're just going to head into the back room here so I can talk to you."

Bobbie was led to the small room, where a narrow window cast a patch of sunlight on the wood floor. When Bobbie felt a wall behind her, she leaned against it. In order to hide their trembling, she locked her hands together behind her back. Jeff had taken her glasses, so until he leaned, with his forearm on the wall above her head, his face nose-to-nose with her own, she could not see him clearly.

"Will you kiss me again, Bobbie?" The question was whisper-soft and Bobbie searched Jeff's eyes for why he would be teasing her in this way.

"Why?" It was the only word that would come.

"Don't you want to?"

"You know I do." Bobbie's heart was in her eyes, and she did nothing to hide how wonderful it was to have Jeff so near. But it wasn't right. "Please don't torment me, Jeff. It's not like you to be cruel."

"I'm not doing a very good job with this, am I?" He said the words almost to himself, and Bobbie was more confused than ever.

"May I have my glasses back?"

"Are you going to run away?"

"I might."

"Then no, you may not," he stated without moving. "And by the way, Sylvia left town this morning. She's headed home to stay."

Bobbie was silent, digesting this newest information.

"Now will you kiss me?"

"You want me to kiss you because Sylvia left town?" Bobbie felt like her world was spinning.

"No," Jeff said with great patience. "I want you to kiss me because you're going to be kissing me every day for the rest of our lives and we need the practice."

Bobbie's hands came up and grabbed at the front of Jeff's shirt. "Please give me my glasses, Jeff."

He complied, and Bobbie searched Jeff's face from behind her lenses. *This is why God told you to trust Him,* Bobbie said to herself as she clearly saw the love in Jeff's eyes.

"Why, Bobbie—why has it taken us so long to see what everyone else has seen for weeks?"

"I don't know," Bobbie answered, and truly she didn't. "Do you still want that kiss?"

Jeff's eyes narrowed with emotional fervor, and that was enough answer for Bobbie. Her hands framed either side of his face and she kissed him tenderly on the lips. Bobbie would have broken the kiss after a brief moment, but Jeff's arms had come around her, causing her own to slide without prompting around his neck. She returned his kiss with every drop of longing she had ever felt.

May he kiss me with the kisses of his mouth!
For your love is better than wine.

Song of Solomon 1:2

Budding Adoration

The men sat quietly as Amy played, each one letting the music flow over him and basking in the sound of Amy's God-given talent. Grant's head lay on the back of his chair with his eyes closed, a slight smile on his lips.

Paul studied the small hands that moved so effortlessly over the keys and produced such celestial sounds, making him think of the way music might sound in heaven.

Silas' eyes never left Amy's face. He studied her lovely arched brows and the slight flush on her high cheekbones. His love found her flawless and lovely beyond compare.

Amy was nearing the end of a beautiful old hymn when she allowed herself to look about the room. Paul had joined Grant in tipping his head back and closing his eyes, but Silas was watching her, his expression loving.

Something inside of Amy began to open and grow, like a small flower beginning to bloom in the warm spring sun. *He's so wonderful and kind, and he loves me.* The real truth of this fact hit Amy for the first time. The knowledge gave her such a warm, secure feeling she felt tears sting her eyes. Silas was God's child and she was God's child and together they could have a wonderful life with His blessing and beneath His watchful care. Unbidden upon the heels of this miraculous thought surfaced the doubts. "Could it really be that wonderful? Would he really love me for the rest of his life?"

Had Amy been able to tell Silas of her feelings and her fears, he would have answered all her questions and assured her of his love.

My heart is steadfast, O God, my heart is steadfast;
I will sing, yes, I will sing praises!

PSALM 57:7

Those Eyes Say a Lot

It took several minutes before the door opened. Ross had begun to think he had been forgotten. Mandy came in and plucked a coffee mug from one of the hooks on the wall, nearly dropping it when she turned to find him standing there. She put the mug on the table and stood still, content just to look at him.

Ross hadn't even been given time to take off his hat and coat. Mandy watched as he pushed his hat back on his head, his eyes seeming to memorize everything about her. She watched as he stripped the glove off one hand and beckoned to her with the crook of one finger.

Mandy didn't need to be asked twice. She walked slowly toward him and stopped when she was close. "I forgot you were invited here today," she said softly.

"I figured as much," he answered, equally soft. "I didn't spot you in church until after I'd sat down, and then the pew filled up and I couldn't come up and sit with you."

"I figured as much."

No other words were necessary as Ross slipped his other glove off and tossed it toward the table without taking his eyes from Mandy. His hands came up to frame her face, his thumbs gently tracing Mandy's cheekbones. Her eyes slid shut at his touch and then flew open when his lips brushed hers.

"Am I out of line?" he questioned her softly, his eyes holding hers.

"No," she breathed as she raised her face invitingly, her eyes closing once again.

Ross needed no further prompting. Both of them were surprised a moment later to see that Silas had come into the room. No apology was made, and Ross slipped his arm around Mandy as they turned to face Silas.

Silas stood for a moment and looked at them. He knew in that instant what other people saw when they looked at him and Amy—a couple in love.

"Hello, Ross." Silas put his hand out and Ross shook it. "I hope you'll stay for coffee."

"I will, thanks."

Mandy saw the gesture for what it was: approval. She left Ross' side and went on tiptoe to kiss Silas' cheek. He hugged her close and then teased her about the coffee she was supposed to be bringing him.

Within minutes the kitchen was filled with Camerons, Nolans, Jacksons, and one Beckett. They were all waiting for coffee or hot chocolate. They were snitching the spice cake that was supposed to be enjoyed with the coffee, as well as the sliced apples that had been put on the table.

Becca plopped down in Ross' lap and gave him bites of her apple. He kissed her cheek on one of those occasions and her little hand flew to that spot as she looked at him with adoring eyes.

Mandy was pleased to see that the man she loved was accepted and loved by her family. When Levi got a bigger piece of cake, Ross traded with Clovis to avoid an argument. It was a little thing really, but everyone noticed and appreciated his thoughtfulness. His eyes, when anyone spoke to him, were attentive and respectful, but no one could help notice the change in them when they turned to focus on Mandy.

They said she was the most wonderful, beautiful, desirable woman on earth and that he loved her. They said how important she was to him and that he cared for her happiness and welfare.

And Mandy's eyes said no less to Ross. She looked at him as if he were the answer to her prayers. And as a life mate, he was.

How beautiful you are, my darling,
how beautiful you are!
Your eyes are like doves.

Song of Solomon 1:15

A Man in Love

The cool air felt wonderful as Smokey stood above the beach and listened to the pounding of the waves against the shore. The nearly full moon sent a ray of light across the surface of the Atlantic that was mesmerizing, shining and winking at her like a thousand tiny jewels.

She felt more than heard Dallas' presence behind her on the grass and turned to find him approaching. He stopped beside her and stared at her for a long moment.

"Did I tell you that you look lovely this evening?"

"Thank you, Dallas. I was thinking you look wonderful too."

Again Dallas stared at her. "I've never before waltzed with a woman, but right now I wish there was music."

Smokey smiled at the very thought and then at herself. "I'd probably step on your foot."

Dallas smiled in return. "With your little feet, I wouldn't even notice."

Smokey chuckled softly, a sound that sent a shiver down Dallas' spine.

"Now how would you be knowing about the size of my feet?" she wished to know.

Dallas' vast hands came up, and he held his fingers about seven inches apart. "You forget I've sailed with you. Your boots are only this big."

Suddenly Smokey didn't feel like laughing. It seemed such an intimate, tender thing to have Dallas know the size of her feet. The thought of leaving him, perhaps for the better part of the year, felt like a knife in her side.

Smokey watched as those hands came forward now to frame her face. He made no move to kiss her, but she felt his thumbs stroke gently over her cheekbones. His eyes in the moonlight were warm and intimate like a man in love.

O Lord, You have searched me and known me.
You know when I sit down and when I rise up;
You understand my thought from afar.
You scrutinize my path and my lying down,
and are intimately acquainted with all my ways.

PSALM 139:1-3

Faith

Open Your Heart

The closing hymn was led by Silas. His voice was deep and clear. In his closing prayer, he asked for God's healing hand upon Pastor Nolan and for those who had not yet accepted Christ.

Once back in the wagon, Silas managed the reins, with Grandma Em sitting beside him. Christine slid forward from her place in the backseat until her face nearly touched Grandma Em's shoulder.

"Grandma Em?" Emily shifted around in her seat with an expectant smile on her face. "You told me your husband, Joseph, was on the other side. Did you mean heaven?" At Grandma Em's nod she went on. "He believed in Christ and you think he is in heaven?" Again Emily only nodded. "And you also believe in Christ and believe you're going to see Joseph when you die?"

"With all my heart, Christine."

It was Christine's turn to nod. Placing a cool hand on Christine's flushed cheek, Grandma Em spoke through tears. "I know you are searching, Christine. I also know that God is your answer. God loves you so much, and I'm praying, Christine, that you will open your heart to that love."

Even though the horses were at a crawl, they were already pulling up to Grandma Em's house. Unlike on most Sundays, everyone including Luke and his guests had arrived ahead of Grandma Em, so she decided it was best to let things go for now.

"If you want to talk later, Christine…" she let the sentence go unfinished. Grandma Em hugged Christine and then Silas was helping her from the wagon. Christine watched as she hurried toward the house.

Christine was preoccupied when Silas helped her down from the wagon. So she was doubly surprised when Silas gave her a big hug. The embrace broken, Christine stood staring at him with wide, surprised eyes. It took a moment for her to realize that in Silas' own quiet way he knew she was hurting.

If you confess with your mouth Jesus as Lord,
and believe in your heart that God raised Him from
the dead, you will be saved.

ROMANS 10:9-10

Preparation of the Heart

A GATHERING OF MEMORIES

How many years had he known Sarah? Ross guessed it must be more than 20; most of their lives. She had always been special. When he'd made a decision for Christ a few years ago, he wasn't long in understanding that any girl he might feel serious about would need to have the same heart for God as he did. There was enough of a change in him that the next time he saw Sarah, she'd eyed him speculatively and asked him what was going on. He didn't immediately answer for fear of wording things wrong and turning her away forever.

But he need not have worried because the Lord was working in Sarah's heart and she came right to his house to pin him down a few days later.

Ross was surprised speechless when, upon explaining to Sarah about his new life in Christ, her eyes filled with tears and she asked him to pray with her. There was no hesitation then, and Ross walked on a cloud for days.

Neither one saw this as a sign for a future together, but being in each other's company was easier all the time with the newfound faith they shared. They often met together in excitement to tell some new biblical truth they'd discovered.

In time Ross did take these things to be a sign that this was the wife God had for him.

But as for me, I will hope continually,
and will praise You yet more and more.

PSALM 71:14

Hungry for God's Word

up rolled to her side and let her gaze roam out the window. The bed was too low to allow her to see anything but sky and trees, but somewhere beyond the glass she heard a mourning dove call to its mate. Pup never heard this sound in Denver, and this morning it made her want to lie in bed all the longer. So often when she came home she was filled with energy and determination to get things done, but today her heart was quiet, her body still. Last night she had been too tired to do anything save fall into bed, but this morning she wanted to pray.

I didn't know I could feel so secure. I didn't know I could be so sure. You're here. You're really here with me, and I know it. I believe this with all my heart, Lord God, and I see now more than ever before that You were here all along. I was wrong to go my way and live my own life. I hadn't thought about my childhood experience with You in so many years, but I know You tried other things to get my attention. I ignored them. That was wrong. I can see this now. Thank You for taking me back.

Pup felt her heart lift with her confession and realized that the last time the Lord had tried to arrest her attention had been while she was burying Govern. What an awful day that had been, and only two-and-a-half months past. Pup remembered her heart had felt as if it were going to burst, but she had pushed the pain away. She had desperately wanted someone here to share the loss and agony with her. She saw now that God had gently revealed to her that He was there for her, but Pup had not really understood or stopped to listen. Now her ears were open wide.

It's nice when we feel good, Callie. Mr. Harrington's words from one evening around the dinner table came back to her with startling clarity. *But our faith must be based on truth. No matter what we're feeling, good or bad, it's to be discarded if it's contrary to God's Word.*

It was then that Pup knew she needed a Bible. She could have kicked herself for not checking the reading room or even the general store when she'd come into Boulder yesterday. The thought of going back down to town did not thrill her, but she would do it if that's what it took to get a copy of the Scriptures.

Percy's face flashed into her mind so swiftly that for a moment she was completely still. A second later the covers were tossed back and she was jumping out of bed to climb into her clothes. Her boots were only half-tied when she went out the front door, gun in hand. Not caring if Mud and Percy were up or not, she moved swiftly toward their place. If Percy didn't have a Bible, she'd head to town. However, something told her he did have one, if not two, and she was just going to have to figure out how to talk it away from him for a time.

Your word I have treasured in my heart,
that I may not sin against You.
Blessed are You, O LORD; teach me Your statutes.

PSALM 119:11-12

Joy
and
Laughter

God's Promises Sink In!

As soon as Cash left, two of the ranch hands came forward to help Reagan down, but she told them she could manage. When she caught sight of one trying to get a glimpse of her ankles, she became all businesslike. In a matter of minutes the job was done, and the men were thanked and sent on their way.

"Did you give them cookies?" Katy asked when Reagan told her of the episode.

"They weren't looking for cookies," Reagan stated in no uncertain terms, and Katy chuckled.

"You can laugh all you want, Katy, but I could have done without them."

Cash, who had just entered the room, exchanged a look with Katy, both sets of eyes holding laughter.

"So how was Lavinia?"

"She misses you and sent you some powder."

"Now wasn't that nice! What scent?"

"Wildflower, I think."

"Mmmm…" Katy showed her appreciation after Reagan had handed her the tin and she had opened it enough to get a whiff. "Who else did you see in town?"

"Before Reagan fills you in," Cash inserted, "I saw Pastor at the livery, and he wanted to know if the three of us are planning to have a Bible study together. I told him we hadn't gotten that far."

"I want to," Reagan said without hesitation. While reading her Bible that morning, she'd had several questions.

"I do too," Katy added.

"All right. We'll start this week. How's Thursday night—in here after dinner?"

"What will we study?" Katy wished to know.

"I'm not sure just yet. Do you have an interest?"

Katy looked thoughtful. "I missed some of the work Pastor Ellis did on God's promises. Can we go over that?"

"Sure. Is that going to work for you, Reagan?"

"Anything," she told him. "I feel completely lost in the Bible."

"Okay. Thursday night it is." Cash went on his way, and Reagan turned to Katy. "Did you talk to him about your doubts?"

"No, because I remembered what he would say."

"What would he say?"

"That all feelings have to follow the truth of Scripture. If I don't feel saved, but I know in my heart that I took care of things between God the Father and me, then I'm saved forever."

"You know so much, Katy," Reagan said in amazement. "How do you know so much?"

Katy did not look pleased. "I sat in that church just trying to be good enough to get God's notice without admitting that His way was the only way He would accept. I did my level best not to listen, but a few things got in!"

Reagan bit her lip in an effort not to laugh, but it didn't work. A giggle slipped out, and then another.

Just realizing what she'd said, Katy began to laugh as well.

Before many moments passed, the two of them were having a loud session of laughter and giggles.

Yield now and be at peace with Him;
thereby good will come to you.
Please receive instruction from His mouth
and establish His words in your heart.

JOB 22:21-22

A Ham in the Family

In strode a man, who without a glance in Christine's direction went to the washstand. Christine stood still, her eyes taking in dark hair and a full, dark beard. His shirt tightened across a broad back and muscular arms as he reached for the soap. His height made him a Cameron.

As he washed, and without looking up, he began to speak in an exasperated voice. "Gram, those pigs are a nuisance. How you stand it is beyond me! And that goat! I was ready to nail his mouth shut this morning. Plus I made the mistake of going out to the pigs before giving corn to the chickens. They followed me and kept up a steady stream of chatter the whole time I was wading in to feed those two monstrosities you call pigs."

Silas Cameron turned from his washing to see he was not addressing his grandmother. He did not know this woman who stared at him as if he had lost his mind, but he was warm to his subject, so he continued. With little more than a flicker of surprise showing in his deep blue eyes—eyes that must be a Cameron trait, Christine thought—he went on.

"Have you seen those pigs?" he asked her directly.

"Belle and Betsy?"

"Right. Well, I'll tell you this family could be eating ham and bacon for years if she'd let us butcher those two. Everyone tried to tell her when she and Grandpa bought this place, but no, she said she felt sorry for the animals and Grandpa never could tell her no. So here we are, how many years later still taking care of—" He stopped when he saw his grandmother standing in the doorway, an amused smile playing across her lips.

Silas was always much quieter than his brothers and sister. He was not one you interrupted—for fear of shutting him up, never to know when he would start again.

Emily now openly smiled at her grandson. Silas returned the smile as he moved over to bend and kiss her cheek. Straightening, he leveled a look at Christine.

"Gram, introduce me to this poor girl who was forced to stand here and listen to me rant and rave."

After the introduction, Silas shot another question at Christine.

"What do you think of Belle and Betsy?"

"Well, they do grow on you."

Christine watched him throw back his head and roar with laughter, giving her a glimpse of beautiful white teeth amid his bearded face. His eyes were still sparkling with mirth when he said, "Grow is something Belle and Betsy do very well!"

This brought laughter from both Grandma Em and Christine as they laid out breakfast. While they ate, Emily couldn't help but notice how relaxed Silas was with Christine. Since he was normally quiet around people he didn't know well, she couldn't help but wonder if he was drawn to her because of her resemblance to Julia or if he was attracted to her as a woman. She was lovely and sweet. Grandma Em ate her breakfast with a thoughtful heart.

Out of the ground the LORD *God formed every beast
of the field and every bird of the sky,
and brought them to the man to see what he would call them;
and whatever the man called a living creature, that was its name.*

GENESIS 2:19

Sibling Tales and Teasing

The meal for Morland's birthday was a smashing success. The family gathered in great humor to celebrate, and the conversation turned to younger days at the Steele home.

"I don't remember that, Edward," Cassandra told him in no uncertain terms. "I think it was you and Lizzy who sneaked into Mother's room and tried on jewelry."

"I would never do such a thing," Lizzy protested, but she received no sympathy. Indeed the table erupted with laughter and disbelief. Nevertheless, that particular episode was debated for some time. Not until there was a slight lull did Tate get a word in.

"Come now, Henry," he urged. "You've not dragged any of your secrets out. Let's hear them."

Henry smiled and said, "I was angelic, didn't you know?"

If the laughter had been loud over Lizzy's declaration, it nearly shook the room over this. Without missing a beat, Henry's siblings took delight in reminding him of some of his escapades. For such a serious child, he had been a bit wild as a young teen.

"If I recall," Lizzy put in, "Henry got in the most trouble for being on horseback when he was supposed to be home."

"I think you're confusing me with our dear sister, Charlotte," Henry said.

"Not fair, Henry," Morland admonished. "She's not here to defend herself."

"Well, then, let's trot out her deeds," Edward suggested. "We can blame it all on her and make ourselves feel much better."

"What I wish to know," Cassandra interjected, changing the subject completely, "is if Charlotte and Barrington sent you a gift, Morland?"

"Yes," the guest of honor answered.

"What is it?"

"I didn't open it."

Cassandra looked surprised.

"But you must!" she proclaimed, and heard her husband start to laugh. "You never mind, Tate! Now listen to me, Morland—a present that arrives by post must be opened on the spot."

"But it came two days before my birthday," Morland explained.

"Have you not heard these rules about birthday gifts, Morland?" Tate interjected. "She has quite a number of them."

"They never worked on Mother," Henry reminded his sister. "She always made you wait."

"And I have forgiven her," Cassandra said piously, putting the room into laughter once again.

Cassandra looked across at Tate, who was smiling hugely at her, her look of innocence changing to laughter with the rest of the family.

Lizzy suddenly pushed her chair back, gaining everyone's attention.

"All this talk of gifts has made me excited. Shall we, Morland?"

He smiled by way of reply as all came to their feet with plans to exit to Ludlow's largest salon in order to watch Morland open his birthday presents.

There also you and your households shall eat before
the LORD your God, and rejoice in all your
undertakings in which the LORD your God has blessed you.

DEUTERONOMY 12:7

Grace
and
Hope

Accepting a Gracious Gift

"What types of things are you shopping for, Mrs. Weston?"

"Lenore," she corrected before going on. "I'm shopping for your trousseau, Anne. Did Robert not tell you?"

Anne looked at her husband, her memory serving that they were going to shop but nothing about his mother's involvement or a trousseau.

"Have I overstepped?" Lenore asked, looking a bit concerned, her gaze going from one to the other.

"Not at all, Mother. I didn't explain to Anne." As Robert turned to do this, he found his wife's face very pale.

"I'm sorry," he immediately began. "Mother wrote and asked me what type of wedding gift would suit us. I told her the first thing that came to mind, and that was that she could take us shopping when we visited London."

"But a trousseau," Anne argued. "It's too much."

"Can you name me one thing you don't need, Anne?"

The question was asked gently, but feeling very humbled and put in her place, Anne gave a swift shake of her head and lowered her eyes to her plate.

"I just remembered I must see Cook about something," Lenore put in at that moment. "Do excuse me, will you?"

"Anne, I'm sorry," Weston wasted no time in saying. "I should never have spoken to you like that in front of my mother."

"Do you think she found me rude and ungrateful?"

"No, I think she found me forgetting my tongue and you embarrassed because of it."

Husband and wife stared across the table at each other.

"Give me your hand," Weston requested. He waited for Anne to reach across the table.

"If you have needs now and we can afford to see to them, or if my mother is offering a gift, why not take care of them?"

Anne reclaimed her hand and shrugged helplessly, her heart unsure of what to do.

"No one will buy anything today that you don't want." Weston cut into Anne's thoughts with this suggestion.

Anne looked uncertain and countered, "Why don't you decide what I should get?"

"If I do that," Weston began, a smile peeking through, "you'll have the trousseau."

Anne's hands came up in exasperation before she said, "Weston, do you not think a few dresses and something more permanent for our home would be a better wedding gift?"

"Our home is full of treasures," he reasoned. "My mother is delighted to shop for you. If we give her full rein—something I fully intend to do—you'll be the best-dressed lady in all of Collingbourne." Weston put his hand up when Anne opened her mouth to speak. "I know that's not your goal in life, and I was being more facetious than anything else, but you do have needs, my mother loves to shop, and she wants to buy us a wedding gift. I find that a perfect combination."

"I did say that I wanted you to decide," Anne said thoughtfully. "It sounds like you have."

Weston's eyes began to smile. "You might even have fun," he teased her.

Anne shook her head in self-derision. "We chased your mother from her breakfast."

"She'd be willing to give up eating for the day if you accept this gift from her." Weston's voice was quiet and gentle.

"Do I need to apologize to your mother? I think I might."

"No, she understands you were taken by surprise, and if you recall, she turned directly to me to find out why you didn't know. She understands who's to blame."

"This getting to know each other will take years."

Weston nodded. "Yes, but I think it will be worth our effort."

Anne silently agreed. It was already worth it to her. Almost daily new things unfolded, new things about herself or her husband that were helping her learn and grow. She believed God had blessed her all the years of her life, but never had His grace been so visible.

An excellent wife, who can find?
For her worth is far above jewels.
The heart of her husband trusts in her,
and he will have no lack of gain.
She makes coverings for herself;
her clothing is fine linen and purple.

PROVERBS 31:10-11,22

Hoping for a Bride

"Cash," his mother said to him much later that night, after the rest of the family had started to head off to bed.

"Yes?" Cash grabbed the serving tray for his mother and walked it into the kitchen. He hadn't planned to linger, but she caught him before he could leave.

"It's time you got married," she said without warning. If Cash hadn't contained himself, he would have laughed.

"Why is that?" he managed, a small smile coming to his mouth.

"Well," she tried, her brow furrowed a little as if she expected him to already know. "I was just watching your brothers with Libby and Darvi tonight, and I thought, 'I want that for Cash too.'"

"I appreciate that, Mother, but sometimes it's easier said than done."

Virginia looked thoughtful. "I suppose it is." Her eyes shifted around the room, gazing lovingly at the contents before looking back to her son. "Between this house and the ranch house, I prefer the ranch house. Did you know that, Cash?"

"No."

Virginia smiled. "You father built that ranch house for us. This house was already built. I love the kitchen at the ranch house and all the rooms. I love the way it's laid out. We've had some great times in this house, and I wouldn't want to move back to Texas, but I do miss that house." She looked Cash in the eye. "But even with all of that, I have no problem with another woman living there. I want you to marry someone who will enjoy the ranch with you. I want your children to grow up there, as you boys did."

Cash so appreciated his mother's words, but he couldn't exactly promise to give her what she wished. He just smiled and stayed quiet.

"Well, dear," she said quietly, in what Cash knew to be her *mother's voice,* "when the time comes, remember that your mother will be delighted."

"Thank you, Mother," he said sincerely, knowing no end of relief that she didn't expect to hear a plan to make this happen. And her eyes, just before she hugged him, told him how deeply he was loved. He took himself off to bed, his heart wondering if God was trying to tell him something or if Dakota's wedding had just put everyone into a matrimonial mood.

> *Make me know Your ways, O Lord;*
> *teach me Your paths.*
> *Lead me in Your truth and teach me,*
> *for You are the God of my salvation;*
> *for You I wait all the day.*
>
> Psalm 25:4-5

Saved by a Stranger

SEAN DONOVAN

It was a sobering experience for Sean to hear the hammers pounding nails to form the gallows where he would meet his death. Sean's window did not look out onto the building site, but as the sun passed its midpoint in the sky, a shadow was cast across the ground, giving a perfect outline of the tall structure that would see his execution.

Sean's hand rose involuntarily to his throat as he lay down on the cot. "I know Your arms are waiting to hold me on the other side, Lord, but the thought of that rope around my neck terrifies me."

The words were whispered, and tears stung Sean's eyes. "Please help me to be strong. I don't know if I've ever given You the glory for anything, but I want to now."

And such were Sean's prayers through the long afternoon. Since he knew his system would hold nothing, he hadn't eaten a thing since before the trial. He was, in a sense, fasting and praying, and God's immeasurable peace had settled upon him. Duncan had come and talked to him again that morning and then prayed aloud, thanking God for the opportunity to know Sean. It had almost been the younger man's undoing.

Having dozed off before Duncan came to get him, Sean shook his head to clear his mind and held his wrists behind his back for cuffing.

Sean's heart, which had been beating at normal speed, began to pound when he saw the crowd around the scaffolding. It had never occurred to him that people would care to witness such a gruesome spectacle, but there was indeed quite a crowd gathered, and it was painful to have to walk through the midst of them to his death.

The walk up the steps of the scaffold was the longest of Sean's life. He was momentarily surprised to see the judge waiting for him on the platform, but a second later he stepped onto the trapdoor and felt the rope tighten around his neck and all other thoughts vanished.

"It's been recently brought to my attention that a document needs to be read at this hanging. For some of you it will be new. For others, it'll jog your memory from many years ago. But either way I assure you, it is legal and I will hear no discussion to the contrary."

The judge cleared his throat and began to read. "As official of this legal hanging in the State of California, in the County of Tulare, I hereby proclaim that for the offense of bank robbery, Sean Donovan will be hanged by the neck until dead. *Unless*, in said case, a woman of good standing in the community—that is, not being a woman of ill repute, a child beater, or an adulteress— will hereby step forward and claim said prisoner to be her lawfully wedded spouse from this day forward."

The announcement was met with gasps of shock and outrage from the throng. An ominous silence followed.

"And since I know I've taken you all by surprise, I'll read it one more time."

Sean would have sworn that nothing but the sight of his Savior would have been able to pry open his eyes, but when the judge began reading the document again, his eyes flew open and he swiveled his head as best he could to look at the man next to him.

Sean was so busy staring at him that he didn't hear a woman calling from the crowd. Murmurs of "Charlie" came to his ears, but the name didn't really register.

Sean watched Duncan's face in disbelief as the sheriff loosened the knot and lifted the rope from his neck. Spots danced before his eyes.

"Don't pass out now, Sean. Charlie has just agreed to marry you."

Sean's eyes went from the grinning sheriff to the judge, who was staring down the steps of the scaffold to a woman standing below. Sean followed his gaze and saw black spots again. With Duncan's hand gripping his arm, he was brought back to his senses just as the judge addressed him.

"Well, son, it seems there's been a change in the plans. Can you stay on your feet long enough to be married?"

I cried with all my heart; answer me, O LORD!
I will observe Your statutes.
I cried to You; save me
and I shall keep Your testimonies.
I rise before dawn and cry for help;
I wait for Your words.
My eyes anticipate the night watches,
that I may meditate on Your word.
Hear my voice according to Your lovingkindness;
revive me, O LORD, according to Your ordinances.

PSALM 119:145-149

Marriage

Love's Perfect Timing

They stood for a moment longer and then Rigg bent and placed a soft kiss on Kaitlin's forehead. Her heart nearly burst at his tenderness. But she wasn't prepared for his next words.

"Kaitlin, I'm in love with you." The words, spoken in Rigg's soft, deep voice, were humble and sincere.

"Oh, Rigg," Kate breathed, wanting to tell him of her love also but being so unsure of her future, she held back. "If only I knew—"

"Shhh." Rigg's voice was gentle as he stopped her. "You don't need to say anything. But I wanted you to know how I felt, and I want you to be secure in my love, not intimidated by it."

Once again Rigg kissed her brow and then placed his arms around her. Kate held tightly to him, thinking that nothing had ever felt so wonderful.

We need to be together, she told the Lord as Rigg pulled away from her and climbed into the wagon. *He loves me and I love him. I've prayed so long to know Your will. Show us Lord, show us Your path for our lives. Give us Your blessing, heavenly Father, to build a marriage in You.*

As though he could read Kate's mind, Rigg prayed as he drove home. He too longed to be with her and felt it was God's will. Rigg sternly told himself that he needed to bide his time in pursuing her. In the light of his belief that it was God's will they be together, he needed to wait for God's timing.

Wait for the LORD;
be strong and let your heart take courage;
yes, wait for the LORD.

PSALM 27:14

Lonely Without You

Once at the station, husband and wife sat quietly waiting for the train to arrive. For a time, both were content to sit and watch the train station activity.

"You will come home to me, won't you, Marcail?"

Marcail turned her head as they sat on a bench by the ticket office and gave Alex a quizzical look. "Where else would I go?"

"You might not *go* anywhere. After I leave, you might find you like it better here and—"

"I'll come home," Marcail quietly cut him off. She'd never seen Alex look as hesitant before and found it rather heartbreaking.

"I think," Marcail added, hoping she was not being overly bold, "that the bed will be lonely without you."

Alex wished he could take her in his arms, and his eyes told her as much. "My bed at home is lonely without you too."

Marcail nodded, finding she was unembarrassed for the first time. Nothing more was said since the train was now coming into the station. Alex stood and pulled Marcail around to the quiet side of the ticket office. Without warning, he pulled her into his arms and kissed her as he'd done on the beach in Fort Bragg.

When Alex was finally on board, Marcail stood on the platform and watched the train as it eased out of sight. She found herself wishing she'd followed her heart. If she had, she would have been on the train with her husband.

Love is patient, love is kind and is not jealous;
love does not brag and is not arrogant,
does not act unbecomingly; it does not seek its own,
is not provoked, does not take into account a wrong suffered,
does not rejoice in unrighteousness, but rejoices with the truth;
bears all things, believes all things,
hopes all things, endures all things.

1 CORINTHIANS 13:4-7

Worth Every Reflection

S tacy knew the evening was going to drag with Tanner away, and a long soak in a tub filled with scented salts was just what she needed.

Supper was delicious, but by the time Stacy finished, she missed Tanner so much she didn't know how she would pass the evening. She opted for a book from the library and was headed that way when he came in the front door. Not caring in the least if the servants were watching, Stacy flew into his arms.

"I missed you," she told him as he bent so she could put her arms around his neck, pressing her soft cheek to his. It took Stacy a moment to realize she was not being hugged in return. He dropped a kiss on her nose before she moved back in order to stare up at him. She stood back and looked at her husband, whose arms were behind his back.

"I missed you too," Tanner told her as he straightened, but Stacy's mind was now on his arms.

"You're hiding something."

"Indeed I am."

Stacy tried to move around him, but Tanner simply moved with her and kept his secret concealed. Stacy finally stood still again and faced him.

"Is it for me?" she asked with a smile.

"Quite possibly," Tanner answered and Stacy saw how much

he was enjoying this. She put her own hands behind her back and simply stared at him.

"Did you stay busy today?" Tanner asked.

"Yes," Stacy said simply, but couldn't stand the suspense any longer. "Do I get to see what it is?"

"Are your hands clean?" Tanner asked, sounding much like a parent. He ruined the effect, however, when his eyes lit with suppressed laughter.

Stacy, like an obedient child, brought her hands forward for his inspection.

"You've been digging in the dirt, haven't you?"

"Guilty as charged," she told him and joined his inspection of her chipped nails.

Tanner gave a deep, mock sigh and brought a large box out from behind his back.

"I'm not sure this is fitting for an urchin like yourself, but here it is."

Stacy's eyes widened in a way that Tanner loved, and he held the bottom of the parcel while she removed the lid and drew forth an exquisite gown.

"Oh, Tanner," Stacy breathed. "It's lovely."

"This is to replace the one you don't like."

Stacy held the dress out in front of her and stared. The dress was a very pale pink silk with snow-white lace. The skirt had multiple gathers at the waist before falling straight to the floor without ruffle or layer. It was the most wonderful gown Stacy had ever seen.

Gently hugging it to her, she spoke. "I'm going to save this for something very special."

"Anything you wish," Tanner told her, feeling inordinately pleased at her response. He really had thought about her way too much, but she was worth every reflection.

My God will supply all your needs according to
His riches in glory in Christ Jesus.

PHILIPPIANS 4:19

Bedtime Conversations

How do you think Jennings and the children are doing?" Lydia asked Palmer. With their children in bed, they were alone in the small parlor for the first time in a long while.

"They seemed very content."

Side by side they sat quietly for a time, Lydia gazing across the room, Palmer watching Lydia.

"You're worrying," he accused her.

"How do you know that?"

"Because I've kissed your neck twice and you haven't noticed."

Lydia turned to look at him. "Have you?"

"Yes." Palmer was amused now.

Lydia turned her gaze back to the room.

"All right. Do it again. This time I'll pay attention."

A smile lighting his eyes, Palmer leaned and kissed her ear and then her shoulder.

"That was nice," Lydia said.

"I was hoping you would think so."

Mrs. Palmer turned to look at him, working to appear as innocent as possible.

"I was worrying, so I think we'd better do something to get my mind off of Jennings and the children."

"A game of whist?" Palmer asked, his eyes as serious as he could manage.

Lydia laughed and put her arms around him. Palmer held her right back. The last thing they needed at the moment was a card game.

Let your fountain be blessed,
and rejoice in the wife of your youth.

PROVERBS 5:18

Peace

Watching for the Dove

Stephen had never been so frightened in all of his life as Bracken and Helga prepared his sister, Megan, to give birth.

Bracken and Megan were confident, calm even, but Stephen nearly came undone. Megan did not understand what was so frightening, but when Bracken left them for a time, Stephen began to talk.

"What if you die?" There were tears in the young man's voice. Finally Megan understood.

"Then I'll live forever with God," she told him serenely.

"Oh, Megan." Stephen's tone was tortured. "To have such assurance must be a wondrous thing."

"You can have it as well, Stephen."

"Nay, Meg, not I." His look was heartrending.

"Yes, Stephen, you. Trust me. I would never lie to you."

The words were a turning point for Stephen. He respected Megan as he did few people. He was ready to listen for the first time, and by the time Megan's baby was born, Stephen was a new creature.

Bracken and Megan were alone as soon as they were able. They sat before the fire in the bedchamber for many minutes, not speaking but getting silently reacquainted.

Finally Megan said, "What is to become of us, Bracken? In truth, I am frightened."

"There is no need. God makes kings, Megan, and He is still in control of England. Our God is the king of the universe."

"Then you are never afraid, Bracken," she stated, her face turned up to see him.

"I would be a fool not to be alert, my love, but I fear not for tomorrow. Has God not proven to us repeatedly that He will see to our every need? Has God not proven His love over and over?"

"Yes, Bracken, He has. I am not trusting."

"Then I will pray that your trust increases."

Megan smiled at him again and put her head back against his arm. He never made light of her shortcomings or rebuked her harshly, but with love and tenderness led the way by word and example.

"You've grown rather quiet," Bracken commented. "Are you worrying?"

"No, not this time. This time I must leave it with God. This time I must trust completely."

Bracken turned her so she was in his arms and he could look down into her face. "In the Holy Scripture a dove is at times the symbol of peace. You're my dove; did you know that, Megan?"

"Oh, Bracken." Her eyes sparkled at his praise. "I love you so."

His head lowered to better place a gentle kiss upon her lips, but he stopped to say one more thing.

"There are no guarantees concerning tomorrow, Megan, but believe as I do, my dove. God alone holds England in the palm of His hand, and as long as He gives me breath I shall be here for you."

"Thank you, Bracken."

"For what?"

Megan smiled, thinking that God had outdone Himself the day He had created her knight, but she didn't answer, and Bracken knew that enough had been said. The duke's head lowered once again and this time he kissed his precious wife so tenderly that words were no longer necessary.

Be anxious for nothing, but in everything by prayer
and supplication with thanksgiving let your requests
be made known to God. And the peace of God,
which surpasses all comprehension,
will guard your hearts and your minds in Christ Jesus.

PHILIPPIANS 4:6-7

Peace in All Things

The sun was up and warm in a cloudless sky when Cassandra arrived on Friday morning. Hastings told her at the door that Tate was already on the veranda. Cassandra headed that way.

"Hello, Mr. Tate."

"Hello, Cassandra. Can you stand to be outside today?"

"Yes. I might have begged for this if I'd found you inside."

Tate waited for her to sit and then handed her the book he'd been holding.

"Here you go."

"What's this?" Cassandra looked down at the new volume.

"Our next book. Have a go at it."

A moment later Cassandra's laughter bubbled out. She didn't know if it was Japanese or Chinese, but she knew one thing: She couldn't read it.

"Where did you unearth this?"

"Hastings is very resourceful," Tate answered with a broad smile, clearly pleased with himself.

"And what if I'd been able to read it?"

"Ah, yes, that would have been fun. The joke would have certainly been on me."

Cassandra laughed a little more.

"Are there other languages you can speak?" Tate suddenly wondered. He was as good with Italian and French as Cassandra was, but until that moment assumed there was nothing else in her repertoire.

"Now that would be telling," Cassandra hedged. In truth, any other language she'd worked on was sketchy, but she didn't want to admit to that just yet.

"You choose to remain a mystery."

"For the moment."

"I might have to keep searching for books."

Cassandra laughed and reached for the nearby paper. "Do you want me to read now?"

"That's fine."

Cassandra held the paper but didn't open it.

"Mr. Tate, may I ask a question of you?"

"Yes."

"How do you pray for yourself? How do you stay at peace when you don't know what will happen with your eyesight?"

"I pray that I'll keep trusting."

"So the biggest issue for you is trust?"

"Yes. It helps that I was studying Moses at the time of my accident. God asked Moses to trust Him in so many ways. Sometimes he failed, and other times he was obedient. But what stuck out the most to me was God's plan in Moses' life. Clearly God knew what He wanted from Moses and how best to take care of His servant.

"As His child, I believe that God has a plan for me. God knows whether my having my sight restored will bring Him honor and glory. I can't tell you that it wouldn't be an adjustment to remain in darkness, but if I need to stay blind in order to be more pleasing to Him, I can't fight that. If I don't thank Him for whatever He has planned, I'll be miserable and fruitless. I fail in my efforts—every day I fail—but my goal is to be righteous and trust Him."

Cassandra found herself oddly choked up. Had she just met this man, all he'd said might have sounded like a lot of religious platitudes. However, she felt confident that he meant every word. She'd been with him for days, seeing his calmness, his sense of peace, and even his effort to put others ahead of himself.

"Are you still there, Cassandra?"

"Yes." She couldn't disguise the thickness of her voice. Indeed, tears were very close. She forced them back. "I'll read to you now."

Tate didn't comment. He had no idea his thoughts would affect her, but he found it strangely comforting.

No man will be able to stand before you
all the days of your life. Just as I have been with Moses,
I will be with you; I will not fail you or forsake you.

JOSHUA 1:5

The Wonder of Answered Prayer

SEAN DONOVAN

I n the beginning was the Word, and the Word was with God, and the Word was God. The same was in the beginning with God."

Sean could read only the first two verses from the book of John before his eyes filled with tears. He knew Charlotte—Charlie—had supper on the table, but he felt an urgency to spend a few moments in God's Word. He bowed his head and prayed before he left the room. Sean thanked God for his life, his wife, and his family before his mind swung back to Charlotte and dwelt there.

"I don't know if this is love, God," he whispered, "but I care for her so much. Please help Charlotte to understand that she needs to know Your Son personally. Please save her and use us to Your glory."

The moment these words were out of his mouth, Sean envisioned them leaving for Hawaii. He stood from his kneeling place next to the bed and gazed out the window like a man in a trance.

"Back to Hawaii! Oh, God," Sean cried softly, "could that thought be from You, because nothing would make me happier than for me to return to Hawaii with Charlotte, so we could work with Father."

Sean took a moment more to give his future to God and in doing so felt an indescribable peace fall over him. He knew he couldn't tell Charlie how he felt, but he also knew that if the thought *had* come from the Lord, He would work it out.

"Sean," Charlie called from outside the door. He'd taken more time than he thought. He opened the door to see her waiting in the hall.

"Are you all right?"

"I'm fine, Charlotte. I was reading my Bible. Did I keep you long?"

"No, but I did wonder what had happened to you."

Charlie talked as she led the way to the supper table where the young couple sat down and ate. Their conversation was light. Then over dishes, Charlie brought·up a subject that nearly made Sean drop the plate he was drying.

"I think we should go to church in the morning."

Sean didn't answer for a moment, and Charlie turned from the dishpan to look at him. "What do you think?"

"I'd like that, Charlotte, if you're sure."

"I'm sure. I think we should go to Duncan and Lora's church."

"That sounds fine." *Fine* was not the way Sean was feeling. Ecstatic, overjoyed, or elated better described his mood, but he wasn't sure he would be able to explain himself to Charlie if he suddenly began to do handstands in the kitchen.

These things I have spoken to you, so that in Me
you may have peace. In the world you have tribulation,
but take courage; I have overcome the world.

JOHN 16:33

Family

The Legacy of Laughter

Coffee was served on the front porch as a lovely breeze blew away any remaining mosquitoes. Grandma Em and Preston had the younger people laughing with stories from their days as kids.

"We were such rascals," Preston began as the evening neared an end. "I remember when I was about ten we decided to put a snake in the teacher's desk. Well, I was the idea man, and none of the other boys ever seemed to notice that I came up with the plans but never got my hands dirty, so to speak.

"Well, I was the delegator on this job and for a very good reason: I'm scared to death of snakes—always have been. I instructed a particular boy to find the snake, and set the time everyone was to meet at the schoolhouse. Then under the guise of watching for the teacher, I stayed well away from the actual snake handling.

"It was 'long about midmorning and I guess we weren't very bright, because it never occurred to us that the snake could get out of the desk. The teacher had opened her desk several times and still there was no scream.

"I remember it was right in the middle of spelling. Faith Lambert, the best speller in class, was up front, and I looked down to find our snake curled up, calm as you please, right next to my foot.

"I came out of my chair as though my pants were on fire and nearly jumped into the lap of the kid in the next desk. It didn't take long for the teacher to catch on for whom the snake was meant, and she knew who the instigator had been. At the time, I didn't recognize the look, but I realize now what a terrible time she had keeping a straight face when she said there would be no punishment because she was sure I'd learned my lesson. I thought the other guys would never let me live it down."

Everyone had tears of laughter on their faces as they pictured the dignified Preston Culver jumping through the air in fear of a snake.

"You wouldn't get along very well with Levi, Mr. Culver," Mandy told him. "He loves snakes. The last one he found he named Henry and wanted to keep it in the house. I thought Amy was going to faint."

"And I thought Silas would be in a heap of trouble," Carrie added. "He laughed about the whole thing after the boys went outside. Amy wasn't very happy with him. She made Mandy check the boys' pockets for days after that."

Our mouth was filled with laughter
and our tongue with joyful shouting;
then they said among the nations,
"The LORD has done great things for them."
The LORD has done great things for us; we are glad.

PSALM 126: 2-3

Letting Go for Love

I want you to be wherever God leads you. As much as I'd miss you, I know Evan and Bev would take good care of you."

"But Dad, what about you? Who would take care of you?"

"Amy, honey, you must not build your life around me. What did you think would happen to me when you and Thomas moved into your own home—that I would wither up and die?"

"Well no, but, Dad, I just figured that the breakup with Thomas was God's way of saying, 'Stay here and take care of your father.'"

"Amy, do you really think me that selfish? I've been where you are—young and ready for love, and I found that love. Your mother and I loved one another deeply, and when God gave us you, there wasn't anything more in the world we would have asked for.

"I want you to experience the things that I have—marriage and family. I can't imagine a man wanting a more wonderful wife than you would be. And when it comes to babies, well, I've seen your face light up when you hold them at church.

"You know I'll respect your decision about living in town or not, and there are no words to describe how much I would miss you if you go. But Amy, do not, *do not* base your decisions on a need to stay here and take care of me."

"But it's not just that. This is a good life here. I love it on this farm."

"You're right—it is a good life. We've been blessed many times over. But God may have a completely different plan for you, Amy, and I'll not hold you back."

There was silence in the room for a long time. Grant's compassion for his only child was great and even though his words had shocked her, they needed to be said.

Amy stood. "I'd best get to the barn."

Grant nodded.

Amy hesitated and then walked to his chair. They hugged long and hard. "This is the only home I've ever known."

"I know, honey, and I'm not pushing you out, but please don't close your eyes to what God might have for you beyond these acres."

Amy stepped back and held her father's hand. She squeezed gently and said, "Thanks, Dad."

*You shall love the LORD your God with all
your heart and with all your soul and with all your might.
These words, which I am commanding you today,
shall be on your heart. You shall teach them diligently to
to your sons and shall talk of them when you sit
in your house and when you walk by the way and
when you lie down and when you rise up.*

DEUTERONOMY 6:5-7

A Restored Family

The meal that evening was very relaxing. Tanner was most charming, and he made Stacy and Drew laugh on more than one occasion. When it seemed that Drew was finished with his dinner, Stacy petitioned God for help one last time and plunged in.

"I have something special to tell you tonight, Drew," Stacy began, knowing she had to do this in her own way. Only her fear that Drew would be hurt in some way by the news gave her the boldness to handle it as she saw fit.

"Do you remember my telling you about baby Moses?"

"He went in the water."

"That's right. Did Moses have a mother and a father?"

"I think so."

"Yes, he did, because that's God's way. How about Adam and Eve in the garden? They had children, didn't they? A mother, a father, and children make a family."

Stacy paused when Drew needed a drink, and then asked, "Who is your mother, Drew?"

"You, Mumma." He smiled as though she were making a game.

"That's right. Who is your father?"

Stacy didn't know which was more heartbreaking, the confusion in her son's eyes or the yearning in her husband's.

"Lord Richardson has the same name as you, doesn't he, Drew?"

The little boy looked at Tanner and then back at Stacy. "His name is Tanner Richardson and your name is Andrew Tanner Richardson. That's because Lord Richardson is your papa."

"What about mumma?"

"I'm still your mumma," Stacy swiftly assured him. "I always will be, but now you have a papa too."

When Drew looked back at Tanner, the duke smiled at him. Drew smiled in return, and Tanner reached forward and brushed the hair over his forehead. Drew's grin broadened, although Stacy wasn't certain he actually understood. Stacy doubted that Tanner was as calm inside as he appeared, but she was thrilled with the way it had gone.

Conversation started up again among the three of them, and whenever Drew started to call Tanner sir or lord, someone would gently correct him. Stacy wasn't certain as to how much he was beginning to understand until it was bedtime.

"Would you like Papa to carry you to bed?" she asked.

Drew's eyes flew to Tanner's, and Stacy's smile was huge as Tanner swung his small son up into his arms.

"Off we go, son." It was as if it happened all the time.

Stacy nearly floated into Drew's bedroom. They were going to be a family! Tanner was not what you'd call warm to her, but he didn't seem quite so angry.

Thank You, Lord, Stacy silently prayed. *Thank You for giving us another chance. Please help us to make the best of it.*

> *We know that God causes all things to work together*
> *for good to those who love God, to those who are*
> *called according to His purpose.*
>
> ROMANS 8:28

Strength and Character

No More Pretending

Dallas pulled the buggy to a halt and shifted in the seat to see Kathleen.

"What's going on, Kathleen?"

"My mother," Kathleen began but did not go on.

"I get the impression that she desperately wants you to marry."

"She does, Dallas, and I would love to be married, but not her way—not through pretense and deceit."

"Pretense?" Dallas was adrift. "I'm not sure I understand."

"Ask me anything about ships, Dallas," Kathleen blurted in anger. "Go on…ask me…ask anything you wish. I've done extensive reading on the subject. Or maybe you'd rather know about the pyramids. I was reading a book about them before you picked me up this evening." Kathleen blurted the words out, forgetting her promise to her mother.

Dallas could only stare at her as she came to a stop and tears flooded her eyes.

"My mother," she whispered tearfully, "believes that all men want a wife who's a little bit stupid and very clingy. She's been teaching me since I was a child that if I want a man, I can't let anyone know I am intelligent."

The tears were flowing freely now, and after Dallas produced a large white handkerchief, he slipped his arm around her. She sobbed into his shoulder, and Dallas said nothing, only listened as she told the truth for the first time in years.

"I don't know if you remember Harvey Blanchard, but we were seeing each other last year." Kathleen was developing a hard case of hiccups, but continued to unburden her heart. "I admire Harvey more than any other man I've ever known. He's brilliant and sensitive and I fell for him our first time out. At first I thought he might be feeling for me as I did for him, but Mother insisted that I play dumb, and quite frankly he was bored out of his head with my wide-eyed looks and inane chatter."

The memory was so painful for Kathleen that she sobbed anew. Dallas didn't know when he'd heard anything so foolish as to pretend ignorance to attract a man. What rot!

"I made a decision tonight." Kathleen lifted her head and attempted to repair her face. Her voice shuddered some, but Dallas could tell that her mind was resolute.

"My father is always telling me to be myself, and now I'm going to be. He's always up when I get home. I'm going to tell him that I'm done pretending and that I'm going to stand up to Mother."

"I'm glad you told me, Kathleen. I hope your parents see your side."

Kathleen's eyes were filled with peace as she answered, "Thanks for everything, Dallas. By the way," Kathleen went on, unable to remember when her heart felt so light, "does Smokey know what a wonderful husband you're going to make?"

"I don't know," he said with a grin for the compliment. "I can't ever get that girl to stand still long enough to listen to me."

"That's part of the problem isn't it, Dallas? She's not a girl, but a woman who knows who she is and what needs to be done. Unless I miss my guess, the very thing that frustrates you is also what you admire the most."

Amazed at her insight, Dallas stared at her. "Did Harvey stick around long enough to learn that you read minds?"

Kathleen laughed, her first heartfelt laugh in a long time.

Remove the false way from me,
and graciously grant me Your law.
I have chosen the faithful way;
I have placed Your ordinances before me.

PSALM 119:29-30

Following God's Heart

With determination, William Jennings made his way to Blackburn Manor to call on Marianne Walker.

"You are up and about," Jennings said when he was given entrance to the salon and Marianne greeted him while standing.

"Only just," she told him.

"I hope I haven't caught you at a poor time, Miss Walker, but in truth I've come on business."

"Not at all, Mr. Jennings. Please sit down."

"I'm here today, Miss Walker, to ask you to become my wife. I've seen how attached the children are to you, and I think you would make a fine mother. You and I don't know each other very well, but it wouldn't be a normal marriage in that sense because I assume you would be spending most of your time with the children. You would do me a great honor if you would marry me."

Color rushed to Marianne's face before draining away swiftly. She didn't know when she'd been so astounded.

"You pay me a great compliment, Mr. Jennings," she began quietly. "I am very fond of your children, but in truth I'm not certain that my marrying you is the best thing." Marianne kept her voice very gentle.

Jennings' face was expressionless over this, his eyes intent as he listened.

"Honestly, Mr. Jennings, the main reason that I must decline is the difference in our beliefs, and that is a serious enough reason for me that I fear I must refuse."

"Of course," Jennings said civilly, only now seeing that he had not thought through every aspect of this union.

He stood, and Marianne also came to her feet.

"I thank you for seeing me, Miss Walker. I shall take my leave now."

Save for the shaking she could not control, Marianne stood completely still as he left. There was an ache in the region of her heart that was unlike anything she'd ever known.

❧

Jennings found the Palmers in the study. Palmer had been working on his books, and Lydia had paid him a visit.

"Well, you weren't gone very long," Palmer commented.

"No," Jennings replied a bit testily. "It didn't take long for the lady to say no."

"What lady?" Lydia asked, realizing only then that she had no idea where her brother had gone.

"Miss Walker," Jennings said as he dropped hard into a chair. "I asked her to marry me, to become a mother to the children."

"Jennings." Lydia's voice was all at once breathless. "Tell me you did not do this."

"What crime have I committed that you look so stricken? I'm more than able to provide for her. I know she cares for the children. But she mentioned the differences in our beliefs, that my beliefs don't measure up."

Lydia sat down very slowly, her face looking more stricken than before.

"Come now, Lydia. You act as though I insulted the woman by asking her! If she was insulted, then she read something wrong."

"It's not that," Lydia said, just above a whisper, her eyes on the carpet. "Marianne Walker is the closest friend I have. She would not have wanted to say no to you because she does love the children. And she would have wanted to be as kind to you as she could possibly manage. I can't stand the thought of her heart in pain as she chose to be obedient to God and not marry someone who doesn't share her faith."

For the first time, Jennings thought about Marianne's feelings.

Do not be bound together with unbelievers; for what partnership
have righteousness and lawlessness,
or what fellowship has light with darkness?
Or...what has a believer in common with an unbeliever?

2 CORINTHIANS 6:14-15

A Surprise Swordsman

Brandon looked across the table at Smokey, his dark eyes intent on her face.

"Darsey tells me that you fence."

To his surprise, Smokey only smiled and said, "Does he now?"

Brandon inclined his handsome head and failed to notice the look of astonishment on his wife's face. Sunny had told herself she was beyond surprises, but it just wasn't so.

"He tells me," Brandon went on smoothly, "that you hold your own very nicely."

Again Smokey only smiled. Brandon waited, but still she said nothing. Smokey's teacup was halfway to her mouth when he asked the question.

"Will you fence with me?"

Brandon's respect for her doubled as she calmly raised the cup to her mouth, drank, and just as calmly placed it back in her saucer.

"I'd have to change my clothes."

"So would I," Brandon informed her, and Smokey nodded. "In the den, in one hour?"

"I'll be there," Smokey told him. She thanked Sunny for the delicious lunch. When she exited a moment later, Darsey went with her.

"You can't be serious," Sunny spoke as soon as the door closed. Brandon chuckled at her look of horror.

"I'm not going to hurt her, love."

"Are you sure?"

"Quite sure. I've never known a woman who fenced, and I must admit I'm more than a little curious. But let me warn you not to get too settled in. I sincerely doubt it will take long to prove the better swordsman."

◦~∽

Smokey was studying an embroidered hunting scene in the den when the door opened. Sunny walked in, followed by Darsey and then Brandon. Smokey stood calmly, her hands clasped behind her back. She watched both Brandon and Sunny study her and smiled at their expressions.

Sunny, whose look was almost envious, was thinking how well suited Smokey would look at the helm of a ship. Brandon on the other hand, thought she looked ten years old. His face gave nothing away, however, as he opened a case and invited Smokey to select a foil. She chose a sleek weapon with an Italian grip. Carefully weighing it in her hand, she walked confidently to the center of the room.

Smokey watched as Brandon moved toward her. As he came forward, Smokey read something in his gaze. Her own lit with amusement.

"Is that doubt I see in your eyes, Lord Hawkesbury?"

"I must confess that it is," he told her with a grin.

"I'll have to see if I can put your doubts to rest," Smokey responded easily, and just held her laughter.

Fighting his own mirth, Brandon bowed low and straightened.

"*En garde*," he said, and their swords clashed.

Only moments into the match, Smokey sliced one of the buttons from his vest, and Brandon's demeanor, much as the pirate's, changed in an instant. His every sense was alert as his small but worthy opponent parried every thrust. As with Haamich Wynn, Brandon found himself to be stronger, but Smokey was faster.

He also found her gaze unnerving. Her eyes rarely left his. Brandon began to believe she could anticipate his moves before he made them. He feigned moves, tried the offense and then the defense, but to no avail. She was with him every step of the way.

Had he not needed every ounce of concentration, he would have laughed at his own conceit in the matter. Darsey's comment that she could hold her own was turning out to be a gross understatement.

As time passed in the most intense fencing either of them had ever done, each participant began to think of an end. Brandon was drenched with sweat, and his arm was screaming at him. Smokey's own face was beaded with perspiration, and her arm ached as well. She was tiring fast and about to cry truce when Brandon surprised her with a fast lunge and flick of his wrist. He flipped the foil right out of her grasp. They all watched as it spiraled neatly through the air to land beneath the north windows.

Smokey sighed with relief and bowed to Brandon, whose chest was heaving.

"I thank you, Lord Hawkesbury," she said. "You are a worthy opponent."

"As are you," Brandon gasped. "Allow me to apologize to you, Miss Simmons, for ever doubting your skill."

The two smiled at each other, and Sunny let out a small sigh of relieved laughter. She felt completely wrung out, and all she had done was watch.

The LORD is my strength and my shield;
my heart trusts in Him, and I am helped.

PSALM 28:7

Love

The Heart's Journey

Abby was a vision in cream-colored satin as she stood with her hand tucked into the curve of Mac's arm. The chords on the piano sounded their cue, and they stepped forward in unison. Every eye in the room was on Abby, but she didn't notice. Her eyes were locked with those of a tall man at the front of the church, and she didn't even know when Mac released her.

The ceremony was lovely. Silas played the piano and Amy sang a solo—a wonderful song of commitment and love within God's care. Abby felt as though her heart would burst when Paul looked into her eyes and not at her hand as he placed a simple gold band upon her finger. All the words he'd spoken grew just a bit dim compared to the promise of love she read in his eyes.

The atmosphere of the church had been hushed and reverent throughout the ceremony until the end when Paul kissed Abby briefly, only to snatch her back in his arms a moment later and kiss her again. The room broke up with laughter and put everyone in high spirits for the reception to be held at Mark and Susanne's.

"You can scoop Abby up and leave any time you want." It was several hours later, and the words were spoken by Grandma Em, her eyes twinkling.

"Thanks, Gram," he said as he hugged her. "I think she believes it her duty to see that everyone is happy and comfortable."

"That's what makes her a good pastor's wife. But I'm sure you'd agree—today belongs to the two of you."

They stood for a moment watching Abby with two of her Cameron nieces: baby Kate on her shoulder and Elizabeth in her lap. She looked jubilant as her eyes caught Paul's.

"You need some of your own, Paul," his grandmother whispered quietly.

"I couldn't agree more." His smile nearly stretched off his face as he started for his wife.

Abby did feel a little strange about leaving ahead of the others, but Paul had her out the door and on the way to the hotel before she had too much time to protest.

"We're going to be here for a few days, and I think we'll have time to visit with everyone."

"Oh, but I was thinking of you, Paul. It's been so long since you visited with them that I didn't want to rush you away."

"I appreciate that, my love, but like I said, we can see them later." He finished speaking just as they stepped into the hotel and, with the room key in Paul's pocket, started right up the stairs.

All was quiet in the hallway outside of their room, and Paul opened the door before lifting Abby into his arms. The door shut with the help of his foot, and he moved to the nightstand where the lantern stood. Abby struck the match and lit the lamp all from the position of his embrace.

"You could put me down, you know."

"I don't want to put you down."

Abby laughed. She thought he sounded like a little boy whose older brother was trying to take away his birthday present.

The room was bathed with a soft glow from the lantern when Paul sat in the overstuffed chair with Abby in his lap. She snuggled against him, thinking how small and protected he made her feel.

"I love you, Red."

Abby's face was radiant as she tipped her head back to stare up at him.

"You," she teased him, "may call me Mrs. Cameron." Paul's laughter bounced off the walls before he looked into her eyes— eyes filled with love and mirroring his own, eyes that assured him that the long, long road to finding each other had been worth every single step.

> *You have made my heart beat faster...my bride;*
> *you have made my heart beat faster with a*
> *single glance of your eyes,*
> *with a single strand of your necklace.*
> Song of Solomon 4:9

Anticipating a Life Together

The door opened without a knock, and Kate looked up to see Rigg leaning against the jamb. His hands were stuffed into his pants pockets, and his totally nonchalant stance belied the rush of emotions inside him. Kate felt herself blushing as he simply stood and looked at her.

"Do you know how many years I've prayed for you?"

Kate shook her head, unsure of how she was supposed to reply.

"I don't think there is ever a time, Kaitlin, that I walk by those chairs in my store—you know the ones where the men sit while their wives are shopping—without wishing my wife was shopping somewhere in my store.

"And the times I receive an order of dresses, wishing that my wife could be with me when I unpacked them so she could have first pick. Or when the boxes of children's shoes come in, wanting to have children of my own to put those little black shoes on."

Rigg pushed away from the door then and came to the table. He placed his hands on the top and leaned down, his nose almost touching Kate's.

"Do you understand what I'm trying to say, Kaitlin?"

"Yes." Kate felt out of breath. She couldn't take her eyes from the man across from her.

"Then tell me, Katie, will you be that wife? Will you marry me?"

Kate couldn't speak. Her heart thundered with joy and wonderment that he had come to her. She finally managed to nod, searching Rigg's face as she did, to see if he understood.

"I have one more question for you, Kate-love. And it's the last time I'll ask. Hereafter, I'll take my welcome for granted. May I kiss you?"

"Oh, yes." Kate had no trouble with those words at all. Rigg kept his hands on the table and leaned until their lips met. The kiss was brief and gentle. Kate was unsure as to whether or not she'd pleased Rigg and voiced her thoughts as soon as she could speak.

"I've never done this before."

"I haven't either." Rigg's voice was equally as soft as Kate's had been, and once again their lips met. No longer satisfied to remain so far from the woman he loved, Rigg moved around the table to take her into his arms.

When Kate could think once again, she found that Rigg had taken her chair and pulled her into his lap.

"I can't sit in your lap!" Kate laughed and moved away from him. "We're not married."

"But we will be, very soon, Miss Prim and Proper." Rigg followed her right out of the chair and silenced her protestations with another kiss.

How handsome you are, my beloved,
and so pleasant!

Song of Solomon 1:16

A Worthy Object of Affection

Do you think he's cute?" Mayann asked her mother while they were preparing the coffee tray.

"Mr. Rawlings? Yes, he's very nice-looking," Felicia said kindly, but she was not going to do too much encouraging. Mayann was growing up fast, but she was not ready to be in a relationship, especially one with a man Slater's age. Felicia wasn't certain, but she figured him somewhere in his mid-twenties, not to mention the fact that they were still getting to know him. However, Betsy, their oldest daughter, suddenly sprang to mind. Felicia was not about to start pushing her daughter at anyone—she did not want to play God in the matter—but if Slater should show some interest in Betsy, Felicia didn't think she'd have any trouble with that at all. Felicia determined to discuss it with Ross later that evening.

"I think Betsy is in love," Mayann said, her voice a little too loud. Felicia came and put a hand on her daughter's shoulder.

"I don't want you to talk like that, Mayann. If Betsy has feelings for Mr. Rawlings, then we'll deal with that in its time, but don't you start planting ideas."

"All right. But do you think he likes her?"

Mayann had Felicia there. In truth, she had never seen Slater Rawlings give any of the young women preferential treatment. He was extremely polite, a real gentleman, but not at any time did she feel he was playing games with the young women of the church.

"Papa sent me out to help," Tanner, suddenly appearing in the doorway, said. "Do you want me to carry the tray?"

"Thank you, Tanner," Felicia responded, but his question brought her up short. How many minutes had she stood here daydreaming?

Lord, she prayed as she followed her children out of the kitchen and into the living room, *Mr. Rawlings needs my love and hospitality, not my matchmaking skills. Please help me to want his spiritual growth more than a husband for my daughter.*

"So where will we go after Nehemiah?" Felicia heard Slater ask her husband as she entered.

"I think the book of Mark. I try to alternate Old and New Testament books, but before we do that, I have some topics I feel we need to cover. Tell me, Slater, does sharing your faith come easily to you?"

"Not as a rule. I don't know how to open the subject with strangers."

"That's my point exactly. So often I think we try to press Jesus Christ onto someone who has given no sign of interest. What if we got to know our neighbors? What if we loved the people we worked with, without ever mentioning our faith, and then when they noticed the difference in us—*making sure they've seen one*—we lovingly explained why we're different and how they can be different too?"

Slater sat back and stared at him. "I almost want to laugh with the irony of your suggestion. I work with Hank Hathaway, and it's been on my mind to share with him, but he never wants to talk. He never lets me into his world, even a little, and for that reason I just haven't felt free to mention my decision for Christ. You've put it so well. He needs to see a difference in my life first."

Ross Caron nodded, thinking this young man was a balm for his heart. Unless he missed his guess, both his daughters thought he was nice to look at, but that wasn't Pastor Caron's main concern. He believed the church needed strong male leadership. If Slater Rawlings stayed around and continued to grow, he could be a help in leading this church to strength and maturity.

"When did you come to Christ, Mr. Rawlings?" Felicia now asked.

"Less than two years ago. A man I'd been working with talked to me. I had a tendency to search in all the wrong places. Some of my family had come to Christ, but I didn't think it was for me." Slater smiled. "I'll never forget that day. I told the Lord that I didn't think I would be any good as His child—that I could never love and serve Him like my brother was trying to do—but if He wanted a rotten sinner like me, I would do my best." Again Slater smiled. "I was in for quite a surprise. The Bible, a book I had always found dry as dust, became so exciting to me that I couldn't get enough of it."

Slater was on the verge of saying that was just the beginning when he looked over to see the oldest Caron girl—he thought she had been introduced as Betty—staring at him with a dreamy look on her face. Slater smiled at her but stopped just short of pulling at his collar, which suddenly felt tight. Had he been invited over here as a prospective son-in-law? The thought chilled Slater to the bone, until a glance at his hosts put him at ease. They were looking at their daughter, neither one happy, and when the younger Caron girl saw it, she dropped her eyes and turned red. Slater busied himself with his coffee cup and was glad when Tanner changed the subject.

They fellowshipped for the next hour, and everyone, even Betsy after she realized what she'd been doing, joined in the conversation and had fun. Slater left, his heart at peace and very thankful as he rode through town toward Griffin's house.

With labor and hardship we kept working night and day
so that we would not be a burden to any of you...
to offer ourselves as a model for you,
so that you would follow our example.

2 THESSALONIANS 3:8-10

What It Feels Like to Fall in Love

Pup's eyes shone with wonder. "As a child I'd come in faith and believed in Jesus Christ. As McKay talked, all the memories came flooding back. There's so much I still don't understand, but it's been so special to know that I'm truly a child of God."

Camille was silent, as she had been for the last several minutes. The women were sitting in Pup's room upstairs.

Miranda had brought them some coffee and sandwiches, and they'd been catching up for more than an hour. Just a few minutes earlier Pup had shocked Camille by suddenly telling her the story of her conversion. In truth, Camille didn't know what she believed, but never had she been this close to someone who'd had a religious experience. If Pup's eyes could be believed, something had really happened.

"I'm happy for you, dear, but I must admit that I was hoping you'd have more to say about McKay."

Pup laughed softly, her eyes turning dreamy. "He's in love with me."

Camille's eyes were just as soft. "I figured as much. Does he realize it yet?"

"I think so. He said he wants to talk to me."

"And you?" The older woman's tone grew excited. "Do you also want to talk with him?"

"Oh, yes, Camille," Pup's voice was whisper soft. "I've never known anyone like him. And when he hugged me goodbye at the station—" here she had to stop.

This was the first time in several hours that she had allowed herself to remember, and right now it was too much to take in.

"And this was all just this morning?" Camille asked.

"The hug? Yes. He took Carlyle and me to the station, and then we talked while Carlyle bought the tickets." She looked Camille in the eye. "Was it like this for you, Camille? Is this how you fell for Nick?"

Camille smiled. "He came to see my father on business. He was in a suit, so tall and handsome. I was young, only 17, but our eyes met when I brought them some coffee. I was so preoccupied that I burned my hand. Nick jumped to his feet and wrapped his handkerchief around it. I melted inside."

May the Lord direct your hearts into the love of God.

2 THESSALONIANS 3:5

The One Worth Waiting For

C hase," Rusty said gently, putting her hand on his chest. Her hand, her huge eyes, and the softness of her voice all worked to stop him in his tracks. This was who she was. This was the woman he'd fallen for. She did not leave things undone. Chase's chest rose on a huge sigh, and for a moment his eyes closed. He opened them again and found her still staring up at him. Chase stared helplessly back. Carla had been so mild. She'd been steady and quiet and very predictable. Never once had she hid under his desk. With Rusty he never knew what was going to happen from one day to the next, yet he loved her with all his heart.

"Chase?" She spoke his name with soft uncertainty.

"I told myself if you ever called me Chase, I would kiss you."

Rusty smiled and glanced out the door. Quintin was just where they'd left him, his eyes on their every move. Rusty looked back at the man with her.

"We have an audience in the other room."

Chase didn't even bother to glance toward the door.

"He'll have to get used to the sight," he whispered and lowered his head to tenderly brush her lips with his own. It was brief, but oh so sweet, and when he raised his head, he smiled warmly into her eyes. Not able to refrain from touching her, he tenderly cupped her jaw and let his thumb stroke over her cheek. For an instant Rusty's eyes closed. He made her feel so warm and cherished. She looked up at him, her eyes saying the words before she could utter them.

"This isn't the place I would have chosen to tell you," she whispered softly, "but I love you, Chase McCandles."

"This place is fine," he said, his voice low, his eyes drilling into hers. "I'll hear those words anytime you want to say them."

Rusty couldn't speak. Her heart was too full. He was the one.

For of His fullness we have all received,
and grace upon grace.

JOHN 1:16

Faith

Something Special

W hat's Edward like, Aunt Mary?" Niki asked.

"Oh, Niki, he's a dear. Walker has Bible study with his older brother, Henry—another fine man."

"I could tell that Edward had something special, I just didn't know how to ask him about it. He gave me a list of verses from the Bible."

"Do you want to ask me any questions?"

"May I?" Niki looked pleased, turning a little to get a better view.

"Certainly. Should I get my Bible?"

"I don't know." The younger woman looked uncertain all of a sudden.

"Why don't you ask me, and if I don't know I can get my Bible or we can check with Walker."

"I guess my question was over the fact that Edward studied his Bible so much. I've hardly studied the Bible at all. I want to, but I don't. Why is that?"

"When you wrote to me several years ago and told me that you'd trusted Christ for salvation, Niki, what church were you and Louis attending?"

"We weren't."

"Then who told you about Christ?"

"A neighbor. I was miserably pregnant with the boys, and she came to visit me each week. We started talking, and she told me that I could have peace with God. She read the verses to me, and I prayed, but I don't know if it was enough. I still don't know."

"Niki, have you ever heard of the phrase 'proving works'?"

"No, never."

"Good works do not save us. There is no number of good deeds we can do to earn heaven, but after we believe in Christ, we are changed. Good works, or proving works, are what tell others that Christ now lives in us and that we're different."

"Would I have learned this had I gone to church?"

"I certainly hope so. You'll learn it at our church."

"I enjoyed Sunday," Niki suddenly confessed. "There's so much I don't know."

"Do you have a Bible, Niki?"

"No. I've traveled too much. I don't afford myself the luxury of taking books along."

"Having your own copy of Scripture is a luxury, but it's also important. We need to get one for you soon. You need to understand the God you put your faith in, so you know what He expects of you. The way to know Him is to study His Word."

Niki was suddenly back in the coach, traveling from Lisbon to Coimbra and watching Edward read his Bible. He seemed to be a man with such peace and confidence. Niki was certain the cause could be traced back to his reading of the Bible.

By grace you have been saved through faith; and
that not of yourselves, it is the gift of God;
not as a result of works, so that no one may boast.

*For we are His workmanship, created in Christ Jesus
for good works, which God prepared beforehand
so that we would walk in them.*

EPHESIANS 2:8-10

Trusting God's Way

S ilas, why are you driving so slowly?"

Silas answered, his voice a caress. "I'm driving slow, hoping that my wife will tell me what is bothering her before we get to the church."

He heard her sigh deeply and waited, hoping she would at last confide in him.

"I'm not pregnant," she admitted quietly.

Silas brought the team to a complete halt in the middle of the road and turned on the seat to look at her, a look she wouldn't return. He watched her profile for a moment, having known that this month was going to be worse because they'd taken care of their nephew and niece, Joshua and Kate, two weeks ago, while Luke and Christine took a short trip.

"You must be sick to death of me telling you I'm not pregnant," Amy spoke before Silas could say anything. Quietly she added, "Probably sick to death of me too."

He leaned forward and put his face so close to her own she had no choice but to look at him. "You know better, Amy. There is nothing that can change my love for you."

Appearing totally unconvinced, she was shocked with Silas' next words.

"Did you ever think that I might be the reason that we've been married over five years and you've never been pregnant?"

"*What?*"

"I'm serious. Did you ever think that there might be something in me, in my body, and the way I'm put together that's keeping us from having children?"

"No, that's ridiculous."

"Why is it ridiculous?"

"I don't know. I've just never heard of such a thing."

"And that makes it ridiculous?"

They sat in silence for a time, both praying.

"Amy."

"Silas." They spoke in unison and then shared a small laugh. "You go first," Silas said.

"I was praying just now and thinking about what you said, and I don't think it really matters—the whys and whos, that is. It might be that there is something in one or both of us that keeps us from conceiving. Either way, it's God's way, and I'm going to have to accept that. If it were God's will that I be pregnant, I would be.

"I'm afraid I don't remember that as often as I need to, and I'm sorry if I made you feel inadequate in any way. If God has children for us, He will give them to us in His time."

Silas pulled her into his arms and held her close.

"I love you, Si."

"I love you too, and I was thinking the exact same thoughts. I've always believed that you're my gift from God, and nothing on this earth is more important than you are."

Do not let kindness and truth leave you;
bind them around your neck,

write them on the tablet of your heart.
So you will find favor and good repute
in the sight of God and man.
Trust in the LORD *with all your heart*
and do not lean on your own understanding.
In all your ways acknowledge Him,
and He will make your paths straight.

PROVERBS 3:3-6

The Beginning of Faith

You must follow your heart, my dear," Milton told her seriously, "and I hope you will learn to follow after God's heart as well."

"Now that sounds like something Brandon would say," Sunny said affectionately.

"I can believe that. Our beliefs are quite similar. They match the beliefs of my father and grandfather—men who believed their faith needed to be handed down to each generation." He hesitated and then went on softly. "And you, Sunny, what do you believe?"

"I'm not sure I believe that you have to believe anything, but I know some things I don't believe. I don't believe that there is just one God. God comes in many forms, and each one of us must decide which God we want to worship, or whether possibly not to believe in any God at all.

"I don't think any man has the right to tell someone else how to act or live. No one should have that type of authority."

"If no man has the right, my dear, then who does?"

Sunny looked at him in confusion, and then her face cleared. "Well, there have to be laws about murder and such, but not for other, more personal things."

"Does Rand have the right to tell Holly no?"

"Yes."

"Who gave him the right?"

"Well, he's her father."

"So what? That doesn't give him the right to deny her something unless he has an authority that backs up his position as her parent."

Again Sunny looked uncertain and then said softly. "You're talking about the Bible."

"Yes, I am. Even parental authority comes from God, and not just any God, but the one and only living, holy God of the Bible. Your not believing in the one true God doesn't change the fact that He exists."

His words were spoken in such tenderness that Sunny did not feel rebuked. She did feel somewhat confused. What if there really was just one God? Before this moment she had never let her mind even entertain such a belief. There was certainly more to the Bible than she had ever realized, if her family was to be believed.

"Don't take my word for it, Sunny," the duke went on, cutting into her intense thoughts. "When you get home, ask Chelsea for a Bible and read the first book. Genesis means beginnings, and I think you might enjoy reading about how perfectly God planned things."

Sunny nodded and smiled at him. The duke reached with a weathered hand and gently patted her cheek.

The word of God is living and active and
sharper than any two-edged sword.

HEBREWS 4:12

Joy
and
Laughter

Snowballs and Sweet Nothings

Well, look at you two!" Grandma Em spoke to the little boys standing around Mac's legs. "You look like you're ready to brave the snow."

"We're here for Christine," Calvin announced.

"That's right. We're going to show her how to have a snowball fight."

Christine laughed with delight and knelt down to pull both heavily garbed boys into her arms. They both became suddenly shy, and Christine said, "I'll go get ready."

⤚⤙

Charles spoke right out, "You're a terrible snowball thrower, Christine! You haven't hit a thing you've aimed at!"

"Well, she throws it pretty far, though—just not in the right direction," Calvin said in an effort to soften Charles' words.

Christine bit her lip to keep from laughing out loud. The boys were so serious. Charles had generously taken her onto his team against Calvin, but Calvin was killing them. He never missed. Charles was a fair shot, but Christine was awful. She tried to be optimistic.

"Well, it's my first time. Let's try it again." The boys were agreeable and they spent some time building up their arsenal.

"Okay, I think we're ready." With that the war was on in earnest. What Christine lost in throwing she made up for in ducking Calvin's barrage. At one point he took her by surprise and hit her right on the side of the head. She let out a false bellow of rage that had both boys in stitches before winding up like a pro and letting a snowball fly. As usual, her aim was quite poor at best, but she did hit someone, causing all three snowball throwers to become deathly quiet and watch as Luke wiped the snow from his face. Knowing beyond a shadow of doubt that Christine's throw was a mistake, Luke couldn't pass up the opportunity to tackle her into the snow.

Her cheeks were cherry red with the cold and her eyes were bright with suppressed laughter. Her hat was tilted a bit and had snow on one side. Luke couldn't think when she had ever looked more beautiful.

He spoke slowly as he approached. "So this is the way I'm treated when I don't see you for three days!"

"It was an accident. I'm sorry," Christine said on a bubble of laughter.

"Oh, you sound very sorry!" Luke fought his own mirth.

This made Christine laugh harder, and she began to back away. "What are you going to do to me?"

Luke smiled at this question and Christine, a little afraid of that smile, turned and ran. She had rounded the far end of the house and thought freedom was in sight when her legs went out from under her.

Christine rolled onto her back and put both hands up to wipe the snow from her face. When she felt Luke's hands join her own, she looked up to see him kneeling beside her.

It was on the tip of her tongue to tell him what a rascal he was for knocking her in the snow, but he was leaning over her now, his eyes locked with hers, his lips descending.

"Christine," he breathed, his lips nearly touching hers.

"We'll save you, Christine!" The spell was broken. Calvin's gallant cry reached them.

Before the boys could round the corner of the house, Luke helped Christine to her feet. He pulled her into his arms and held her close under the guise of dusting the snow off her back. The boys bounced on to the scene just as he released her.

Even as the boys danced around their legs, Luke and Christine's eyes locked once again. "I'm sorry," Christine said, the words for his ears alone. Luke took her hand and squeezed it gently. "Later," she heard him say. The look in his eyes told Christine it was a promise he would keep.

Like a lily among the thorns,
so is my darling among the maidens.

SONG OF SONGS 2:2-3

An Afternoon for the Imagination

Rusty had never in her life seen a dining room table the size of the one at Briarly. Her brother and sisters would be mad with envy if they could see the fort she was planning to build beneath it.

"We're going to the dining room?" Quintin asked when Rusty turned right at the bottom of the stairs.

"That's right," she answered in a singsong voice. "We're going to make the best fort in the whole wide world."

"In here?"

"Yes, it's perfect!"

Quintin's look was more than dubious, so Rusty just laughed.

"Now, we'll need to cover both ends of the table and this whole side," she instructed, referring to the side nearest the door, "but we'll leave the other side open so we can look out onto the veranda and the garden. Won't that be great?"

Rusty's enthusiasm was contagious. In moments Quintin's hesitancy fell away, and he was helping Rusty throw the spreads over the top of the table and position them just right. Moved gently so as not to scratch, the chairs helped hold things in place, and with the aid of a few more blankets, all was in readiness. Rusty scrambled beneath without a word and waited for Quintin to join her.

It took a few seconds, but the look on his face was worth every moment. With the light coming from the French doors off the veranda, Rusty could see she had delighted him yet again. Short as she was, Rusty sat nearly upright, and as soon as she giggled, Quintin flew into her lap.

"I love you, Aunt Rusty."

"Oh, Quin," Rusty breathed. "I love you. Aren't we great fort builders?"

"Yes." He looked around. "It's dark in here." His voice was hushed.

"Yes, it is. Don't you love it?"

He nodded, his eyes big and bright with wonder.

"Now, you go up to my bed and your bed and gather all the pillows you can carry. I'll find the book we're reading and tell Mrs. Whitley that we *must* have lunch in the fort today."

"Okay." He scrambled out and dashed off to do as she bid. It did Rusty a great deal of good to hear him run up the stairs. Such a thing had been utterly forbidden as she was growing up, but this situation called for new rules and standards. Rusty made her way to the kitchen. As she hoped, she found Cook and Mrs. Whitley.

"Mrs. Whit," she said, "May Quin and I have our lunch under the dining room table today? We don't expect you to wait on us." She always said that. "We'll come and get everything."

"That's fine, Rusty," Mrs. Whitley always enjoyed saying. "But Cook and I will bring everything to you. Sandwiches might be easiest."

"I think so too, and those short round glasses that won't tip so easily."

"Lemonade?"

"Perfect. And cookies, so we won't need forks. Oh! Would you please ask Whit to bring the Gramophone to us? I think we need a little music."

"Certainly."

Rusty thanked them as she always did, making them feel as if they'd made her day, and went on her way. The two older women smiled at each other.

"Have I mentioned that I'm glad she's here?" Cook asked.

He will exult over you with joy,
He will be quiet in His love,
He will rejoice over you with shouts of joy.

ZEPHANIAH 3:17

Undisguised Adoration

C allie Jennings isn't my real name," she added. "It's Andrea May Hackett." She had stunned them again but went on to explain the importance of staying Callie, and keeping her nickname Pup, of course. She also explained her feelings about the way she'd deceived people. Although they'd laughed today over some of her past antics, Callie's decision never to mislead people again was a serious one. Harry and Liz agreed with her wholeheartedly.

"Don't forget the last disguise," McKay prompted her, wishing his parents could have seen her in the costume that had so taken him by surprise. "The one with the blonde wig and maid's uniform."

"Inga," Pup supplied.

"Inga?" Liz asked, eyes still wide.

"Yah. Das me, Inga."

Both Harry and Liz burst out in laughter. Pup laughed with them and looked over to find McKay's eyes fixed on her. She grinned at him, and although noticing his intent gaze, she didn't comment.

"What did Inga do?" Harry asked, as intrigued as he'd been all afternoon.

"She got into the Phipps mansion as a maid. It took a few days to penetrate Duncan's private office, but there was valuable information there. I can't say too much, but the case should be open and shut because of it."

"Oh, Callie," Liz said on a sigh; she looked almost drained. "We had no idea, but we're so pleased that you could tell us."

"I hated not telling you before, and then when I had to leave so suddenly, I thought you would never want to see me again."

"We can't say we understood," Harry told her, "because we didn't, not really. But we weren't angry, and Mickey explained that you didn't have a choice."

"Thank you, Harry. Thank you, Liz." She felt as if a weight had been taken from her shoulders.

"I think we all need a little something to eat and drink. I know I do," Liz proclaimed and stood. "Harry, will you help me?"

"Indeed I will."

Husband and wife exited. They had no more walked from the room than McKay grabbed Pup and kissed her.

"Talk like Inga again," he said when he raised his head.

"I won't," she told him on a laugh, but he kissed her again anyhow. There was little Pup enjoyed more than McKay's kisses, but now was not the time or place. She wriggled from his arms and stood. He reached for her again, but she evaded him, moving around the back of the sofa. McKay stood as well, never taking his eyes off of her.

"Go ahead, Pup," he cajoled softly, "talk like Inga."

She laughed but still refused. He started toward her and she darted away.

"What has come over you, McKay Harrington?" she asked, her eyes huge.

"I just realized how much fun being married to you is going to be," he said softly as he circled the sofa.

"Well, we're not married yet, so you just stay over there."

She was roundly ignored. This time he literally jumped over the back of the davenport to get at her, but she somehow escaped his arms. When they faced each other again, his eyes narrowed and Pup shook her head. She darted toward the front door and all but ran to the kitchen.

Liz and Harry looked up when she entered so suddenly, but she drew up short and gave them a nervous smile, stopping just inside the kitchen door. They smiled in return when McKay followed close at her heels. He wasn't moving as fast, but it was clear who his prey was. They didn't continue to stare at them, so McKay stepped close to her side, slipped an arm around her waist, and whispered in her ear.

"I'll take this up with you later," he warned her softly, and pressed a kiss to her temple. Pup only smiled.

How beautiful and how delightful you are,
my love, with all your charms!

SONG OF SOLOMON 7:6

Gratitude
and
Thanksgiving

A New Creature

God's grace amazed Stacy repeatedly when she thought about the way all her children had come to Him, even though their father had had little voice in the matter for all these years.

Tanner still enjoyed his debates with Brandon, and in fact the four of them had only grown closer as the years passed, but Tanner, to Stacy's knowledge, had never made Christ his Lord. Still she prayed, believing.

"Wool gathering?"

Stacy smiled at the sound of that deep voice and rose to embrace her husband.

"How was your trip?" she asked, their arms still tight around each other.

"Good."

Stacy gave a heartfelt sigh. "That's a relief." She stood in the circle of his arms just staring at him for a full minute.

Finally she spoke. "Tanner, what's come over you? I can't quite put my finger on it, but you seem quite different."

Tanner gently kissed her brow, his look very tranquil.

"I believe the Scriptures call it being 'a new creature in Christ.'"

Stacy stood in quiet shock for the space of several heartbeats.

"Oh, my darling Tanner," Stacy whispered when she could

talk. Her hands came up to frame his face, and she looked at him through tear-filled eyes.

"When did this happen, Tanner?"

"About a week ago," he said, his voice more serene than Stacy had ever heard. "It's been an especially fine year for my investments, and I was sitting in my office congratulating myself as usual for my fine business acumen when it suddenly occurred to me that without God I would have nothing.

"I felt as if I'd been struck. You, the children—everything is from God. He is the Provider and Savior. I couldn't go on after that. I wrestled for some minutes, but I knew I could never again pretend that I had been responsible."

"But how did you—?"

"I've been listening to you talk to the children for years, sweetheart. I prayed and told Him that I believe in Him and need a Savior for my sins. And you well know He never turns anyone away."

Stacy was overcome then. When Stacy could control herself, Tanner began to speak. He told her how empty he'd been feeling inside for the last year and how much he'd begun to think of eternity.

"I'm not a young man anymore, you know. I'm 56 this year and I've lived much of that time for myself. It was more than time for a change, a permanent change."

They talked on for some time, and then Tanner stood, eager to go and share with his family. Stacy opted to stay where she was and watch the scene unfold. She smiled, tears coming to her eyes again as they thronged him, arms hugging amid cries of delight and praise to God.

"I never wanted anyone else, Father." Stacy spoke out loud. "From the moment I laid eyes on Tanner, I knew my heart was lost. Then You chose me, now You have chosen him. In Your love You have given me my deepest desire."

A breeze had come up, and Stacy's words were gently snatched away. Not that it mattered. God had heard them and as soon as her family, who was now coming to see her, arrived, she would gladly say them again.

The LORD is my strength and song,
and He has become my salvation;
this is my God, and I will praise Him;
my father's God, and I will extol Him.

EXODUS 15:2

God Bless Our Friends

Mercy, you two are cute! was all Dakota could think as he watched Calder and Merry's children. He didn't know how long he and Darvi would be in Stillwater, but he thought he could get very attached to these two little girls.

"Dinner's ready," Merry announced from the edge of the room.

The men thanked her and stood.

Calder gave Merry a kiss, and one of the girls went into her arms.

"It smells good," Calder commented.

"Beef stew, biscuits, watermelon, and iced tea."

"Oh, my," Dakota said softly.

Merry turned to him, her eyes sparkling a little. "Don't you care for beef stew, Mr. Rawlings?"

"On the contrary, Mrs. Scott, quite suddenly I'm starving."

Having figured he would appreciate a home-cooked meal, Merry was very pleased. She was even more pleased when she saw that the girls were not going to stare at him all evening and then hide their faces when he looked their way. She was exhausted these days—she suspected she was pregnant—and in her mother's pride, she wanted Dakota and especially Darvi to see the twins at their best.

"All right, girls," Calder spoke after they had sat down. "Whose turn is it to pray tonight?"

"Vivvy's," Pilar was swift to say. "I was before."

Calder smiled at her wording and turned to Vivian.

"All right, Viv. Here we go. Dear Lord…"

"Dear Lor."

"Thank You for the food."

"For food."

"And all Mama's work."

"Mama."

"For friends."

This was met with silence.

"For friends," Calder repeated, his voice prompting.

Still it was quiet.

Calder finally had no choice but to open his eyes and look at his daughter. He found her staring around the table.

"Vivian, can you thank God for friends?"

"No."

"Why not?"

"Where's my friend Beth?"

Understanding dawned. "Not *your* friends. Mama's and *my* friends. We have friends too."

The adults at the table had kept their eyes closed, but each had something over his or her mouth. Dakota's hand covered his upper lip, Darvi used her napkin, and Merry's apron helped her stem the laughter that lingered just under the surface.

"I'll go ahead and finish; you can close your eyes again," Calder stated.

Waiting until Vivian obeyed, the host went ahead with the prayer he had in mind, just barely holding his own laughter. No adults exchanged glances after Calder's amen, which was for the best. It would have been some time before anyone would have been able to eat.

"Do You hear what these children are saying?"
And Jesus said to them, "Yes; have you never read,
'Out of the mouth of infants and nursing babies
You have prepared praise for Yourself'?"

MATTHEW 21:16

Beautiful Day

A Song for Silas

J ulia, you're pregnant."

"I'm what?"

"You are going to have a baby." Mark enunciated the words carefully as though speaking to a slow-witted child.

"But that's impossible."

Mark's eyebrows rose nearly to his hairline on that statement, but Julia rushed on. "I mean, I just never got pregnant after Charlie, and I just assumed I couldn't." Julia's voice trailed off rather helplessly as she tried to take it all in. She was as surprised as Mark that she and Mac had not noticed any of the signs, for they had been there, staring them right in the face.

Mac! Julia's next thoughts were of her husband. She had to tell him right away.

The door leading from the office into the living room opened slowly, and Mac's entire body tensed as he watched his wife walk out, followed by her brother. In his peripheral vision he caught Mark leading Susanne from the room to give them privacy, but his eyes were locked on Julia.

She walked toward him and without forewarning said, "I'm going to have a baby."

Mac's eyes closed, and he felt as if all the air had left his body. He stood a moment trying to pull air into his lungs. *Thank You, God. Thank You, God,* his heart kept repeating.

When at last he opened his eyes, he pulled Julia tenderly into his arms. Julia felt him tremble, and her heart broke. He had been so worried.

The boys found their parents in this embrace and, even though it was not an unusual sight, approached carefully.

When they broke apart, Calvin said, "Uncle Mark says you're okay and that you have good news."

Julia broke the news to them with tears in her eyes. When Mark and Sue heard shouts and laughter from the living room, they knew it was all right to return.

What followed was a joyous chaos of laughter and tears. Mark took Julia back into his office to tell her how to take care of herself and things to watch for. She had never fainted when pregnant with the boys, and he intended to keep a careful eye upon her. He insisted Mac join them as he wanted his orders followed to the letter.

A while later Mac headed the wagon for Grandma Em's. Even with the boys fighting in the back over who would tell her the news, he thought this was probably the most beautiful day God had ever created.

Behold, children are a gift of the Lord,
the fruit of the womb is a reward.
Like arrows in the hand of a warrior,
so are the children of one's youth.
How blessed is the man whose quiver is full of them.

PSALM 127:3-5

Prayer

Led to Pray

SEAN DONOVAN

Katie had been sitting motionless for more than an hour. She knew she would never be able to get out of bed in the morning if she didn't lie down and get some rest soon, but her heart was so heavy with thoughts of her brother, Sean, that sleep seemed hours away.

It had been nearly two years since Aunt Maureen had written, beside herself that he had gone off on his own. They had been forced to accept Sean's decision, but there had been times when it had been close to torture to sit and wonder where he might be.

So why, tonight of all nights, was he so heavy on her heart? Every day she thought of him and prayed that God would guide his path and someday bring him home, but tonight was different; tonight there was an urgency in her thoughts. Something was happening this night, and Kaitlin knew she had to pray.

Rigg stirred in the bed when someone knocked on the bedroom door. Kate, not wanting him to be disturbed, started to rise, but Rigg was already to the door. He opened it and found Marcail, now 14, waiting outside in her gown and robe. Rigg, not understanding why Kate was awake, also wondered at the fact Marcail wasn't sound asleep.

Rigg stepped back and allowed her to see Kate at the window. She moved forward and stopped beside the rocking chair, letting Kate see her face in the moonlight.

"I can't sleep."

"No," Kaitlin spoke softly, "I can't either. Are you worried about Sean?"

Marcail nodded, misery written all over her young face. "Where is he, Katie?"

"I wish I knew."

"Do you think he's in trouble?"

This time it was Katie's turn to nod. "We've got to pray, Marc. God knows all about this, and we're going to give it to Him right now."

The sisters bowed their heads. Each in her own way petitioned God on behalf of their brother.

Marcail, really still just a girl, asked God to keep Sean safe, and to bring him back to Santa Rosa right away so they would know he was all right.

Kaitlin, a mother, prayed differently. She prayed that Sean would make wise choices and seek God's will above his own. She also prayed that God would be glorified in Sean's life, even if it meant her beloved brother would have to know a season of pain.

In the same way the Spirit also helps our weakness;
for we do not know how to pray as we should, but the
Spirit Himself intercedes for us with
groanings too deep for words.

ROMANS 8:26

The Blessing of Being Prayed For

Reagan found herself at the kitchen table set for five, with Alisa's high chair close by her mother's seat. The rolls were directly in front of her, and she was about to take one so she could pass the basket when Russell's voice stopped her.

"I think it's my turn to pray tonight," he said. Reagan was glad she'd not made a move. She bowed her head along with everyone else and waited for one of the memorized prayers she'd heard off and on over the years.

"Father in heaven," Russell began, "thank You for this wonderful day and the way You blessed us each hour. Thank You for all Holly's hard work and this great food we can eat. Thank You that Reagan could join us. What a blessing to have her live in the little house and be such a good neighbor. Bless us as we eat and spend the evening together, and may we ever be mindful of Your presence and blessing in our lives. In Christ's name I pray. Amen."

Reagan managed to raise her head, but the rolls and other food were forgotten. No one had ever prayed for her before. She hadn't even known that a person could talk to God like that. If she hadn't known better, she'd have wondered if Russell might not be a man of the cloth.

*[I] do not cease giving thanks for you, while making
mention of you in my prayers.*

EPHESIANS 1:16

Embracing Childlike Faith

I haven't done enough of this," Pup whispered quietly to God. She walked until she reached the lake and then stood very still, her eyes on the glassy surface. "I remember talking to You as a child, but I just stopped. I didn't know it could be like this. I didn't know I could be so certain. I remember now. I remember so much of what I read that summer in Denver."

She stopped, too full of emotion to go on. Verses and stories came flooding back to her: The lame man who wanted to get into the water, but no one would lift him; the woman who had had five husbands and was living with yet another man; the small man who climbed a tree just to gain a glimpse of Christ. She had gobbled up those stories, but the man she'd been working with had not been like McKay Harrington. He'd been cold and unapproachable. McKay's faith was sincere. And now wasn't her faith too?

"I've had You all along and not really understood. It was suddenly so clear when McKay talked to me. At times I think I had a grasp, but then I was too busy to pay attention. I want to pay attention now, God. I want to be as sincere as McKay is. I want it to be real this time. I want to tell Nick and Camille. The church at Boulder," she suddenly said, "I could go there. The one that Travis Buchanan attends. I could start down on Saturday nights and sleep in the woods until morning. I wouldn't look fancy, but that doesn't matter."

Pup stopped, her eyes closing. Her mind was going so fast she felt she would burst. She turned from the bank toward the lake, tripping on a branch as she went. As usual she never noticed. Something else was on her mind.

> *Teach me good discernment and knowledge,*
> *for I believe in Your commandments.*
> *Before I was afflicted I went astray, but now I keep Your word.*
> *You are good and do good; teach me Your statutes.*
>
> PSALM 119:66-68

Romance

Insider Information

W e're loaded, Captain," Robby reported to Smokey and waited for her orders.

"Thanks, Rob. Tell Pete and Nate they're on watch, and tell Darsey I want to go to Clancy's Place."

"Will do," Robby replied and shut her door. She threw the bolt and began to change. She was feeling rather tired, but it would be some time before she was back here, and even though they were running behind schedule, she wanted to see Bart and Meg.

An hour later the group left the ship. The men knew very well they were welcome to go elsewhere, but they loved Clancy's, so following Darsey and Smokey was more than just habit.

The usual exchange of conversation and coin took place inside, and before long, Smokey and her crew were seated around the back table with plates of food and mugs of tea or ale.

Halfway through the evening, Meg reappeared. She dropped her considerable bulk down at the far end of the table and beckoned to Smokey with one finger.

"A've told Bart he can 'andle things for a spell. I want to talk with me girl."

Smokey smiled at her friend, who wasn't really old enough to be a mother to her but had always treated her with maternal care.

"Where's that good-looking sailor ya had with ya last time?"

"Dallas," Smokey supplied. "He was just with us for the one voyage."

"More's the pity. I thought there might be something a cookin' there."

"Oh, Meg." Smokey laughed. "You're a hopeless romantic."

"*I'm* romantic! Hear her talk!" the older woman exclaimed. "*I* wasn't the one a gawkin' at ya with calf's eyes the whole evenin'."

"He was not," Smokey told her and laughed at Meg's round-eyed expression.

"Ya spend too much time in the salty air, love. He could barely keeps his eyes from ya. In truth, he didn't even try."

"Do you mean that, Meg?" Smokey had grown as serious as her hostess.

"I've been working in this tavern for many a year, love, and I know a smitten man when I sees him. He was gone, I tells ya." Meg reached and tugged the braid that fell down Smokey's back. "And you've never worn your hair down afore this bloke sailed with ya. I says ya feels the same for him."

A huge smile broke across Smokey's face, and Meg cackled with glee. They talked on, fun talk, girl talk.

Kindness and truth will be to those who devise good.

PROVERBS 14:22

A Blessed Union

Dakota's quiet and distracted state before the ceremony had not been the result of second thoughts. Not for a moment did he doubt whether or not he and Darvi should be married. But his heart had been prayerful, asking God to bless this union and help him to be the husband he needed to be. For this reason and many more, he was now able to stand in great joy and excitement and watch Darvi come up the aisle toward him.

Hundreds of people from St. Louis and family from far and wide had turned out to see these nuptials, but the bride and groom were hardly aware of them. Darvi heard someone sniff and thought her mother might be tearful, but she herself didn't want to cry at all. She worked to keep her eyes on Pastor Daniel Cooper, a man she had come to love and deeply respect since her conversion, but her gaze strayed repeatedly to Dakota, who was just as distracted by her presence.

They both grew solemn when it was time to repeat their vows, promises they were taking very seriously, and in rather short order, they were pronounced husband and wife. Mr. and Mrs. Dakota Rawlings turned to face the church and found smiles at every glance. The couple led the way out of the sanctuary to the large hall where a banquet had been prepared. Taking their seats at the head table, they were joined by the family, and the merrymaking began.

Hours later, after good food and lots of hugs and good wishes, the bride and groom climbed into a covered carriage and settled against the plush seat.

"You know," Dakota said for his wife's ears alone, his arm holding her close, "I couldn't help but notice that this dress has a lot of buttons down the back."

Darvi turned to look at him. "It does, doesn't it? Do you think that will be a problem?"

"Not for me." He sounded very satisfied. "I'm a very patient man."

Darvi started to laugh, but Dakota caught it with a kiss before they both settled back to finish the ride to the hotel.

I will rejoice greatly in the Lord,
my soul will exult in my God;
for He has clothed me with garments of salvation,
He has wrapped me with a robe of righteousness,
as a bridegroom decks himself with a garland,
and as a bride adorns herself with her jewels.

Isaiah 61:10

Always

She's not here, Mr. Jennings," Mrs. Walker said. "She took a walk in the park."

Jennings couldn't stop his smile.

"Do you mind terribly, Mrs. Walker, if I don't stay?"

"Well, I do have a lovely new book on flowers I wanted to show you," she said with great regret.

Jennings paused. The two stared at each other until Jennings laughed. Mrs. Walker could not hold the act; her mischievous eyes gave her away.

"Go, Mr. Jennings," Marianne's mother said with a laugh of her own. "And don't come back until you've found her!"

That man had needed no further urging. Jennings knew that if it took the rest of the day, he would stay in the forest until he located Marianne Walker. He'd been riding for less than ten minutes, but it felt like hours. The temptation to call out was mighty, but he held his peace and prayed.

Five minutes later he spotted her dark head. Surprise lifting his brows, he saw that she was in the identical spot where she'd previously hurt her ankle. Sitting on the ridge, eyes toward the valley, she remained rather still. Jennings dismounted and strode toward her. He stood looking down on her, his eyes warm.

"Hello," he said at last.

"Hello," Marianne said, feeling her cheeks heat, although her eyes remained on his.

"This is a familiar place," Jennings commented, amazed at how satisfying it felt just to gaze at her.

"It is," she agreed, "and isn't it ironic—I seem to have hurt my ankle again."

Taking her at her word, Jennings went down on one knee even as he realized she sounded quite pleased about the fact.

"Shall I check it?"

With a swift movement, one that belied an injury, Marianne moved her dress even farther over her ankles and feet.

"There's no need," she said, her voice almost playful as her eyes watched him. "I believe it's already quite swollen."

Jennings worked at not smiling, but one peeked through. Their eyes held for several more lovely seconds before Jennings slowly leaned forward and brushed her lips with his own.

"Do you know what you've been doing to my heart?"

"I think I must."

Jennings kissed her again.

"Will you marry me?"

Marianne sighed quite audibly. "I feared you would never ask."

A moment later she was on her feet and in his arms.

"I'm sorry it took so long for me to come to you. It took me several days to see what I was missing with you."

"You're sure?" Marianne teased him. "I could go away again."

His arms tightened around her.

"I don't think so. I'm going to see your father straight away and have the matter settled."

"What matter would that be?"

Jennings looked deep into her eyes.

"I'm going to tell *him* that I love his daughter and want to make her my wife. And I'm going to tell *you* that there will never be a time when I don't need you."

> *If we love one another, God abides in us,*
> *and His love is perfected in us.*
>
> 1 JOHN 4:12

The Perfection of God's Plan

I was thinking about our wedding day today," Edward said, his eyes on his wife.

Niki looked as pleased as she felt. "I thought about it too."

"As pretty as Penny was, she couldn't compare with you in your wedding dress."

Niki smiled. Edward always had loving things to say, even after all these years. Niki was opening her mouth to say something to him when someone knocked on the door. Edward went to answer it, finding Sunny outside the room, looking for her mother.

"She'll be out in a little while," her father told her, and shut the door again.

Edward looked back to find Niki out of the tub and wrapped in a thick robe. He returned to stand in front of her and took her in his arms. Not needing words, they hugged and kissed for a long time.

Edward decided, not for the first time, that God's timing and will were perfect. He wasn't looking for love when he went to Africa. He wasn't looking for a wife when Niki came across his path, but God, in His imponderable way, had had a plan.

"Edward," Niki said, having caught a look on his face. "What are you thinking about?"

Edward knew he would never be able to explain and said only, "Just thanking God for you."

Niki smiled in her tender way and went up on tiptoe to kiss him again.

> *I thank my God always concerning you for the grace of*
> *God which was given you in Christ Jesus.*

1 CORINTHIANS 1:4

Dear Readers,

What a fun walk down memory lane. It was great looking back at the books from the past and thinking about all of you. Because I write one book at a time and get very wrapped up in the process, it's always a surprise to me to see how long the list has become.

Another surprise to me were the changes—not in the books, but in me. If you've read my books in the past you already know this, but if this is your first, I can tell you there have been many changes. I'm thankful to say—because of God's great mercy—that I'm not the same person. I read things in some of the relationships I've created that I would handle differently today. I hope the same can be said for you. I hope you are letting God mold and change you to His glory.

What has not changed is my love and appreciation for you, my readers. Thank you for the support and prayers over the years. My ongoing prayer is that we will understand what a great, mighty, and holy God we have, and understand that the future will be full of changes and blessings because of His Son's great work of the cross in us.

Warmest blessings in Christ,
Lori

P.S. Thanks, Hope Lyda, for all your work. I hope in the future we can do another book like this.

About the Author

L ori Wick is a multifaceted author of Christian fiction. As comfortable writing period stories as she is penning contemporary works, Lori's books (6 million in print) vary widely in location and time period. Lori's faithful fans consistently put her series and stand-alone works on the bestseller lists. Lori and her husband, Bob, live with their swiftly growing family in the Midwest.

To read samples from Lori Wick's other novels, visit www.harvesthousepublishers.com

Other Books by Lori Wick

The Tucker Mills Trilogy
Moonlight on the Millpond
Just Above a Whisper
Leave a Candle Burning

Big Sky Dreams
Cassidy
Sabrina
Jessie

Contemporary Fiction
Sophie's Heart
Pretense
The Princess
Bamboo & Lace
Every Storm
White Chocolate Moments